T0114837

LOVE
TEACHES
LOVE

NIA RAMSEY

authorHOUSE®

AuthorHouse™
1663 Liberty Drive
Bloomington, IN 47403
www.authorhouse.com
Phone: 833-262-8899

Published by AuthorHouse 02/24/2021

ISBN: 978-1-6655-1741-6 (sc)
ISBN: 978-1-6655-1753-9 (e)

ACKNOWLEDGMENTS

Most writers, when thinking of the many people in their life who in their own individual ways, contributes to the story that she or he manages to tell, probably like me find it difficult to know who to thank first. This was my dilemma at first until I realized how simple it actually was. First and foremost all honor has to go to God, the almighty, whose wisdom and molding put all the people and experiences in my life that helped me become a writer, and whose promise to me from the time I was a little girl, that he was my shepherd and that "I shall not be in want". First he put my mother in my life to give me life and by her example of strength, taught me life lessons of perseverance. She raised me and my siblings basically without any or very little help from others. My father was hospitalized with Tuberculosis when me and my siblings were very young, at a time when there was not yet standard modern treatment for the disease. He eventually died years later, while still in the hospital because of the side effects from the experimental treatment he was given. All during this time my mother gave us kids a home and provided for our needs. She took us shopping at the Goodwill Store where we found fashionable clothes and were able to dress like kids from a two parent household of financial stability. She humbled herself to borrow money from my friend's mother when there was no money for dinner. She received money and help from Welfare and stayed home to raise her five children until we were old enough for her to return to school and get her college degree. I remember the nights she came home after night school with a sweet potato pie for the family as a special treat. It was her voice at a crucial point in my life when I could have made a horrible choice that might have led me down the wrong path. Thank you mom for your guiding voice, sent by God, at that critical moment. I am sorry your life had so much pain, but God knew you were strong enough to be both mother and father to us kids when Satan came against you and our family. I love you.

I thank God for everyone who by their help or example, helped in God's plan to mold me. To my wonderful children and grandchildren, you helped me beyond what I can express. It was God's love that has allowed me to have you in my life and learn from you, that I feel, was the most important part of molding me. Latrise and Dorese, you both showed me what and who I could be. I watched you both with a mother's true amazement of what it is to experience motherhood. It seem at times that you were the parents. I know our lives together has been rocky at times with all that Satan has attacked us with. Your father could have been a better father to you and a better husband to me if not for Satan's interference. Forgive him and me for our weakness as parents. I am sorry our family went through such heartache. Your father's family also went through heartache. Your aunts and uncles love you and me, and your grandparents loved us also. They all did the best they could to show us love. We all went through pain.

But you and your families, in spite of everything, have caused me to realize what life is meant to be. I remember the lesson of protection, when you, Latrise, was choking while drinking your bottle of milk formula when I tried to feed you when I was home alone one day. God directed me to run to seek help from an older mother in the apartment building we lived in. This mother of a family of boys, showed me what to do.

Dorese, I remember the lesson of letting you learn some independence while being close to help you if danger came. I stood watching over you, looking through the peek-hole of our front door, after you had packed your bag with my help, at the age of maybe four. You had declared you were running away from home. I watched you for some time before you got tired of standing outside the door and finally decided to knock on the door to come back in.

Latrise, your love of photography awoke a love for it in me. Dorese, your love of making quilts has inspired me to want to try doing it also.

Jasmine, you were the first grandchild. I was so overjoyed when I saw you for the first time. Yes, you were the first and there are so many visual pictures of you that I have in my mind, along with actual photos of you. I remember taking you for your first professional photos. Such joy.

Then there was Dominique. Dominique, I was so amazed at the inquisitive little girl you were. Alisha I wondered at that same spark in you. I have a photo I took of you both when you two meet each other for the first time. Dominique, you were looking at your little cousin with such interest while you Alisha, looked at Dominique with equal interest and intensity. I laugh with joy every time I see that photo.

Then along came you, R.J., my wonderful grandson, Robert Dewey Eddy III, I watched you with amazement when you used to fling your child's chair around in imitation of the wrestlers you and your dad watched on T.V. I don't know if you remember the times I tried to teach you to read, I was so proud of you.

Then, Kayla, you came along; my youngest and I fell in love with another grandchild when I saw you. I hurt so much that I wasn't able to capture as many photos of you as I did of the others. I no longer had a camera and had lost the spark for taking photos, but you will always have a special place in my heart like all the other grandchildren. I remember the many mornings of taking you to school and proudly watching you walk with confidence into the building. You always seem like an old soul. I remember the many times you interceded, like a trained counselor during the many battles Alisha and I had. She was and perhaps is still a little bit on the stubborn side. You patiently calmed the both of us down when we were locked in a battle of an adult trying to correct a child's misbehavior, who refused to be guided.

The joy of loving you all and the strengthening you all gave me by your love has taught me how indeed God is the source of all that we can need, his divine plan for our lives is so amazing. You all are like a special gift given at Christmas. Thank you all for your love. And thanks to all the other amazing people I have known; my siblings and their families; the many fellow students who went to school with me, I am sorry that I have forgotten some of you; then there were the others like the families I stayed with as a child during summer camp sponsored by the Fresh Air Fund; and there were fellow co-workers on various jobs I had. A special thanks to my brother who taught me to dance and play cards, and to develop a love of books by sharing his books with me. Also for my sisters who each taught me lessons by their support and the sibling interactions we had; there were many. Margarette, as the oldest you taught me how to sketch and I remember you teaching me how to cook potato salad. Edith, I thank you for allowing me to stay with you for a short period when Sonny and I separated. And for encouraging me when I attended Pharmacy School. My sister Jeannie, I thank you for offering me to stay with you when I became ill by being exposed to LSD without my knowledge. I am sorry I didn't accept your offer. I could have been with you when you became ill with cancer. I watched you when you came to New York seeking help from Sloan Kettering Hospital, only to die there. It was painful watching you suffer during my visit to the hospital to be with you.

All the pain of some memories were able to help me feel empathy for the many patients and other people struggling with problems. But the fond memories also helped to realize the beauty of God healing us from our pain. My fondest memory is of singing to my children. Latrise, there is the memory of me trying to coax you to eat as a toddler by singing "Yummy, Yummy, I got food in my Tummy to you. Somehow that worked. Dorese, I could only get you to sleep after feeding you your bottle of formula, by singing the song "Born Free" to you. Again, to everyone who has played a part in my life in God's plan to mold me, I thank you.

SYNOPSIS

The story unfolds with an unidentifiable prophet who is sleeping and receives visions about the beginning of creation and the course leading to its apocalyptic end. The visions show him the horror of the destruction of a world once beautiful and full of potential until destroyed by man's greed and hate. The story tries to convey what can be done on a small individual scale to make life better for all.

The first chapter after the prologue of the prophet, starts with the character Tamara, who is a young, bright Black teenage girl who lives in Williamsburg, Brooklyn with her mother, Ann, who teaches math at a public school in Brooklyn. Tamara, writing in her journal, reflects on the other characters in the story. The story deals with the lives of the characters just before a devastating fire that erupts suddenly in the apartment building where Tamara lives and what happens to the characters after the fire. A portion of the story is told by entries in Tamara's journal. In one section she describes Sarah, an Irish homeless woman, who was formerly once a great ballet dancer in Europe. Through flashbacks, Sarah's life is told and the tragedies that lead to her current psychological breakdown are revealed.

Another character introduced in the story is Kwuame, a Black male teenager who also lives in Tamara's apartment building. Kwuame is Afro-centric, restless and somewhat unfocused about his goals. He has a best friend, Nat, who desires to be a movie director like his idol, Oscar Micheaux. The two friends discuss a wide range of black history; the Black holocaust of slavery, crime, and dealing with racism's effects on the Black youth. They also discuss their aspirations, apprehensions, fears and their desire to know who they are. The young characters will learn that they must get past some of the negative images society has of them so that they don't become a victim of them.

An elderly, retired Jewish couple, the Rosensheins, also resides in the apartment building and are central characters of the story. This couple are still very much in love and display a lot of humor and love of life. One of them will have just successfully battled cancer and survived (the husband). During the fire Mr Rosenshein helps Kwuame (who gets trapped in the burning fire while trying to rescue a grandmother and child) and leads him safely out of the building. But during Mr Rosenshein's assistance of helping Kwuame, he substances some injuries and burns that cause him to be hospitalized. While in the burn unit of the hospital, Mr Rosenshein succumbs to his injuries and dies. Before he dies he will have a heart to heart talk with Kwuame who comes to visit him in the hospital. He tells Kwuame of his war experience and how a Black soldier had saved his life. Kwuame agonizes over the death of this Jewish man who saved his life and the previous anger and distrust he has had for Jews and Whites. After struggling with these conflicts he emerges with a desire to foster racial tolerance in the world and decides to join a group that tries to implement and encourage unity among all racial groups.

Another character in the story, does not live in the apartment building but gets to develop a father/son relationship with an older blind man who does live in the building. This character is a young Hispanic man named Manny, who is the younger brother of a Major League Baseball player. Being the darkest member of his family, Manny faces prejudicial hostility from his mother (at least that is what he believes) - that causes him to have low self-esteem and to embark on a drug and alcohol road of destruction. Fortunately before it is too late, Manny gets help when he enters a community center drug and counseling program. But even more instrumental in helping him to realize his potential and overcome his self-doubts, is his relationship with Raul, the blind man who works part time as one of the counselors at the community center.

Two other characters dealing with fears and confusion are a retired Black grandmother and her daughter, Nettie. The daughter, who is abandoned by her husband for another woman, now lives with her mother and four children in the apartment building. Her mother has just recently retired and is facing fears of growing old and feeling useless. Before dying in the fire, the grandmother will overcome her depression and encourages her daughter about her future and leaves her an insurance policy that will enable her daughter to take steps (finishing school) that will financially help her and she will realize her inner strengths and capabilities as she watches her mother's transformation brought about by her deep faith in God and her belief in his mighty, enpowering Love.

Another central character is John, a White male whose military experience has left him a paraplegic. John literally locks himself up in the small confine of his apartment, bitter and no longer desiring to participate in life. After Manny learns of John's plight from Raul, he tries to help him emerge into society again.

The lesson the characters learn in the story is the power of love to transform our lives and help us deal with our fears, hate and anger so that we can be what God intended us to be and how through love we can teach love to others and as a consequence improve our world.

LOVE TEACHES LOVE

Somewhere in the mist of time, an old prophet dreamt his dreams. World events, some past, some present, and others yet to come, paraded through the recesses of his mind in vast spectrum of colors;Brilliant, vibrant colors intermingled with soft, fleeting whispers of hue to almost stark black and white images, depicting stories some have known, know and will know. Across millenniums these stories traveled to reach the sleeping prophet.

Letters spread out in front of the prophet's tunnel vision, in black and white, forming patterns of ancient tongues. His eyes zoomed closer, trying to decipher the images but the pattern shifted to rise in spirals, moving outwards before compressing together. Inhaling and exhaling the letters into his being, the prophet mumbled the words "In the beginning was the word and the word was with God.." John 1:1, then shifted his body spread-eagled with arms stretched wide as if in welcome embrace.

In brilliant bursts of explosions, the prophet saw the formation of huge magnificent mountains, jagged valleys, the gush of rushing, roaring waters of the murky deep. Earth and sky meet in all their glory in a symphony of music and colors, each offering up their treasures; species of crawling insects, powerful beasts running on all fours, feathery birds climbing up to the heights that their wing-span would take them. Across vast miles the prophet was shown the lush vegetation and natural resources of lands yet untouched.

In the midst of all this beauty, the prophet saw the beginning of man. Man with his awesome potential of unlimited dimensions, stood up and surveyed God's world. Men multiplied and with their kingdoms spread out to the far corners of the world. Soon the prophet watched as the rise of many mighty men swept across lands, plundering, stripping and swallowing up the innocent and the ones caught unaware sleeping at the guard posts. Onward, relentlessly, these men marched, trampling all in their path, on their quest of greed and power. These men lived, died and were replaced by other men more cunning and ferocious in their appetite for wealth of rare jewels, silver, gold, vast mineral riches, choice foods, sexual perversions and consuming power. They plotted their schemes that were brought to life by the misery and death of many people. Prophecies from all ages rushed to the sleeping prophet and scene after scene of world events and mysteries revealed themselves to him. Incredulous in the weight of their immensity and message, these visions brought spasmodic shivering to the ancient body of the old prophet and silent tears spilled from his closed eyelids.

Vague, shadowy, enormous and grotesque figures more frightening than the ruthless men - wailed in shrill intensity, some booming in lead rage, while hovering over each event, pushed with mighty arms, propelling the scenes forward. Soon the prophet was surrounded by these demonic beings who howled ferociously as they caused a whirlwind of catastrophic vibrations that advanced the world in wider spirals of confusion, cruelty and hatred. Blood splattered in Technicolor everywhere across the screen of the prophet's mind. The shivering of the prophet was replaced with violent shakes and jerks as he tried to protect himself from the raging madness spinning around him. The whirlwind created by the spinning events picked up speed as the demons pushed harder and harder igniting eruptions of fires everywhere. Then in fury, the demons hauled the scenes at the prophet. At this point he was in battle for survival. The roar of a mighty explosion threw licking flames and sulfurous black smoke far up past the heights of the clouds and tall buildings within magnificent cities. Hot metals melting from the intense heat, oozed and flowed like hot lava. Thunderous booming could be heard as structure after structure collapsed as the flames destroyed foundations and supporting beams. Exploding glass flew everywhere, cutting with precision those caught in the path of the jagged, splintered edges. There were fires, movement and chaos intermingled everywhere with heart piercing wailing.

The aftermath, a dense foreboding silence, brought the prophet to consciousness and he struggled to lift his exhausted body to a sitting position, his body heaving as he gasped for air, and great sobs tore from his mouth. With deep sorrow he cried in pain for the children of God, and in anguish, feverish prayer, moaned "Dear God, please bring forth the power of your love. Almighty savior, only your love can engulf such hate and wickedness and destroy it." Sluggishly, he sank back onto the comfort of his bed and became still, as he returned once again to unfolding dreams. He felt a sudden blast of cold air and behind closed eyelids he witnessed a group of homeless people gathered around and hunched over a fire burning in a large metal garbage can. The flames of the fire swirled upwards into the pungent, acrid stench of the smoke filled air. Dark, tall, broken structures of once magnificent buildings stood silhouetted against the background sky. They stood, if only for the moment, as the testimony to the limit of the wisdom of mankind and a saga of heroic deeds and self serving, cowardly misdeeds.

The homeless people stood closely together and it didn't matter what race or sex or age they were, because THEY WERE ALL HOMELESS and at this moment trying to kept warm, rubbing their bare hands over the heat as they bounced their bodies in an effort to keep their body temperature from dropping. Old stories from past life experiences; a joke remembered, and wisdom acquired on life's journey, were shared to help past the hours and keep their minds off of the cold.

From within the gathering came a halting faltering small voice,

"I may be wrong but I don't think any great society has ever fallen, been destroyed because they were practicing a perpetuation of love in their lives; love for God, for family and neighbors, humanity. As far as I know from reflecting on what was taught of the past, all the previous societies' great empires, such as the Egyptian, Babylonian, Persian, Mongol Roman and Creek; their downfalls were usually brought about by greed, a quest for power or a proliferation of immoral behavior. Love didn't destroy them, no, they had power but it didn't save them and they had wealth but that didn't save them either. You would think someone would have tried love" the other homeless people nodded their heads and mumbled in agreement.

Incredulous in the weight of their immensity and message, these visions brought spasmodic shivering to the ancient body of the old prophet and silent tears spilled from his closed eyelids.

TAMARA

Briefly, while not quite fully awake, but striving to bring awareness to the forefront of her mind, the teenager Tamara, tried to grasp at the remnants of her fleeting dream of the sleeping prophet. The sequence of events seen by the prophet and the final occurance of the homeless people huddled together, nagged at her. She felt a lingering uneasiness as she considered the dream. A shiver raced up her spine; she wondered if the dream was a hint of something in her future. Cold air prick her arms as a gust of wind blew in through her open bedroom window, further reminding her of the dream. She jumped up from the bed and closed the window. At that moment she heard the voice of her mother Ann, singing in the kitchen and her mood suddenly brighten and the bleakness of the dream faded.

Ann's singing brought a huge smile to Tamara's face. Her mother was singing in her distinct alto voice, a melody that was forceful and joyful that resonated throughout the rooms of the apartment. Her mother's singing was genuinely invigorating. Comforted by the music, Tamara hurried into the bathroom to take her shower. Minutes later she emerged and quickly got dressed. Moving quickly, Tamara arranged her nature hair twists in a pleasing up-style, that complimented her high cheekbone and reflected the style of the fashionable African hair designs she had seen in a Black Natural hair style magazine. After careful examination of herself in her long oval mirror hanging from her bedroom door she was satisfied with her appearance and she opened her bedroom door and walked down the hallway leading to the front of the apartment and into the kitchen.

Her mom was standing near the kitchen sink preparing Tamara favorite pancakes; fluffy, large blueberry pancakes. The coffee was on and its aroma filled the air with a sweet aromatic fragrance. The radio was playing "All the man I need" by Whitney Houston and her mom was singing along trying to hit the high notes, but with her vocal range, unable to quite reach them.

Smiling, Tamara greeted her mom, "Good morning Whitney, you sure sound great this morning".

"Okay, smartie", Ann answered, turning around to face Tamara. "Enough with critiquing me", she smiled broadly then turned back to stirring the pancake batter.

Watching her mom work, Tamara Ramsey, turned quickly and glimpsed at the wall clock and wondered if she had enough time to dive into a subject matter she wanted to discuss with her mother. Yesterday in her creative writing class at Booker T. Washington High School, her teacher Ms Bates gave the class a journal writing assignment. The class had just finished reading "The Diary of A Young Girl" by Ann Frank, and like the main character in the book, a young Jewish girl who had written a journal while she and her family were in hiding from the Nazi during World War II, her teacher, Ms. Bates, wanted Tamara's class to start writing a journal too. She told the class to record daily, if possible, their perception of their lives; past and present and future possibilities. She encouraged them to write about whatever passion, insight and truths they encountered. She said the experience they would receive from doing it could perceivably help shape their future and help to sharpen their creativity. She had then paused and quoted Carl Schurg, "Ideas are like stars, you will not succeed in touching them with your hands. But like the seafaring man on the desert of waters, you choose them as your guides and following them you will reach your destiny", she quoted.

So influenced by Ms. Bates' provocative exhortations, Tamara had decided then to start her journal with reflections about her mom and dad. Today, standing in the Kitchen, she wondered if a discussion about her parents, in order to get information which would aid her in writing an introduction for her journal, would upset her mother. Tamara felt it might elicit a wealth of interesting stories or possibly an eruption of fireworks along with disdain from her mother..It had been about five years since Tamara and her mother had moved to Brooklyn to escape from her dad's dreadful behavior. Married life had stifled her dad and he had used every opportunity to express his discontent; excuse after excuse of why he came home late, dressing up as if for a date but according to him he was just going to be hanging out with the guys. During the years of living with his wife he had cajoled her every chance he got, to overlook the reality of his nightly activities. After years of obsessing about catching some genital infection or Aids from him because of his reckless philandering outside of the mariage, Tamara's mother had had enough. Now with just the two of them living together, Tamara realized that she and her mother were more relaxed and happier without her dad in the family home stressing her mother.

Tamara continued watching her mother and decided to forge ahead and question her mother cautiously.

"Mom, yesterday my English teacher assigned a journal writing assignment for my class. I thought I could write this journal and who knows, maybe sometime in the future it would be read by people of all ages, both sex, all races and every creed, from all over the world". Tamara paused and looked as if she was reflecting on what she had just said. "I visualized giving the World an insight into the mind of a young black female teenager during the era of crack, Aids, rampant homelessness and the angry white male. Some of my friends like Kwuame would probably say that I'm deluding myself if I really think anyone cares what teenage girls think, especially a black one", Tamara looked intensely at Ann. " But irregardless I feel this venture is worth undertaking; maybe in the future we will have a more unified and more compassionate world that is able to view everyone with respect and equality. I thought I would start my journal with a mawkishly rivet depiction of the beginning of our family; you know, woman meets man, gets married, have a baby, then they were a family of three, etc., etc., etc.....", Tamara mirthfully said with boundless glee.

She sat down at the kitchen table and withdrew a pen and one of her notebooks from her back pack that she had left on the kitchen table yesterday. With pen in hand, Tamara waited for her mother' reaction. At the abrupt look of weariness that registered on her mother's face, as she turned around to face Tamara, Tamara instantly wondered with chagrin, if she might have to coax her mother to cooperate in supplying any information for her project.

Ann had stopped stirring the pancakes and had slapped the wooden spoon she was using into the batter.

"Tamara, why do you want to ruin this beautiful day for me. I'm not in the mood to discuss your father." Ann said as her face registered an uneasiness of mind.

"Dad probably hadn't sent his monthly child support payment yet again for the umpteen time", Tamara thought. His noncompliance to the court ordered child support was getting to be a regular headache for her mom.

"Some things in life would take a miracle to redeem and your dad is one of those unfortunately", Ann said tirely. She regretted her words immediately. She knew she shouldn't malign her husband in Tamara's presence and quickly tried to change the subject.

"Talking about miracles, the Board of Education must literally expect teachers to perform miracles, judging by the small, pitiful budget they've given us this year. If I was able to perform miracles, the first one I would do is see that adequate staffing was available in every school, so children would not be forced in over crowded classrooms because there aren't enough teachers. Then I would be certain to supply quality and plentiful books for all students. Yes, I would do this and more", Ann said with an obstinate scowl.

Ann taught fourth grade at Lexington Thomas Dorsey Elementary School, and for Ann and her fellow teachers, things had been horrendous for some time. She had on numerous occasions complained to Tamara that many of the classes in her school lacked enough textbooks for major subjects like math, English, Science and History.

"Now with more massive cuts planned by the city, what are the children going to be left with; empty buildings I suppose?" Ann asked with contempt. After a pause a sparkle of her previous happy mood lighted Ann's eyes and she said,

"Yesterday while talking with Mr Gilman, the owner of that department store near my school, I got a commitment from him to donate a few computers for my math Lab. I was teasing him and told him that the Parents and Teachers Association was considering a boycott of neighboring stores that never donated anything to our school during our fundraising events. Then I said everyone was excited about the possibility of a boycott and we should be able to pass a resolution to start making plans immediately".

"Tamara, you should have seen that man's eyes. They were bulging out like Freddy Kuger had just put one of his switchblade hands on his shoulder. You should have seen how quickly he offered to donate a few computers to the school", Ann bent over laughing and started wheezing. Tamara jumped up and patted Ann on her back to help her breathe.

"Mom, stop. It sure sounds like you can perform miracles", Tamara laughed along with Ann.

"Maybe you are right honey. That man is considered the stingiest tightward to come along in a long time. And to make matters worse, he gets at least twenty-five percent of every family's income in the area.

Her mother was right about Mr Gilman's profit line, Tamara thought. His store practically supplied almost all that a family would need for any occasion, in any season. In the summer it had air conditioners priced for any budget as well as fans to keep you cool. When the fall arrived, there was an assortment of school supplies and clothes to outfit children returning to school. Come winter and Christmas, you could find any gift to put under the tree; from gloves, sweaters to the latest advertised toys. When spring breezed in, neighbors could throw off their winter coats and buy the newest, stylish fashion to be decked out in, that the store had to offer. Mr Gilman's store was also convenient because it was within the neighborhood and people could go there instead of having to travel downtown to the more distant shopping district.

"Now that Mr. Gilman is giving the school computers, I'm going to buy that Math software program I was telling you about", Ann said.

Last week Ann had come home one day excited about a project she wanted to implement in her math lab for her students. It was a software series that dealt with multi-heritage facts that she had seen in a teacher's supplies brochure. This particular software not only taught heritage facts of multi racial groups but also incorporated various aspects of school subjects like math, science, history, etc. The one she wanted dealt with math. This software not only taught math solving skills but also introduced students to ethnically diverse groups of role models who had been proficient in math. Ann had explained to her that the software introduced role models like black mathematicians Benjamin Banneker, David Blackwell, J. Ernest Wilkins and Hispanic mathematicians Richard A. Tapia, Victor Neumann-Lara, Alberto Calderon, Jose Chain. Ann felt the software program would help to build self esteem and foster an appreciation of other racial groups in her students. Tamara knew that was what captivated her mother most about the program. She felt that knowing other racial groups achievements helped to boost tolerance and respect for others among people.

At the time her mother had initially mentioned this software, Tamara hadn't bothered to ask her whose money she was going to use to purchase this item, she had already known the answer. Ever since her mother had been teaching she had dipped into her own savings to be able to supplement the inadequate supplies that the Board of Education provided for the classroom. She always told herself and Tamara that she would put in for reimbursement in spite of knowing the reality of the futility of this ever possibly happening. Tamara had learnt to not point this out to her mother who would only become defensive and spend her money for the supplies anyway. Her students were like family to her and Tamara knew that if she wasn't so sure of her mother's affection, she might find herself jealous of those snotty nose little students. A big grin spread across Tamara's face and she said,

"Mom, you really care deeply about your students and their education, don't you?"

"Tamara, I just want to encourage them to accomplish all their goals and to excel in life. It's my desire to give them tools that will help them learn skills that would aid them in achieving that accomplishment", Ann said as she came over to Tamara and hugged her.

"Now, how about you helping me make breakfast?"

"Sure, Mom, I'll whip up some omelets okay?"

"That would be great darling. Add some onions in mine."

Tamara crossed over to the corner where the refrigerator was and opened it, then took out a box of eggs, a packet of mild cheddar cheese, a green pepper and a plastic container containing chopped ham. She placed them on the counter next to the stove. Together, Tamara and Ann worked beside each other preparing the meal. Soon they both joined in, playfully singing with the singers on the radio as they went about making their Saturday morning breakfast. When finished, the two sat down at the kitchen table to eat. Ann looked at her daughter as they ate and thought about her ex-husband, Jack, and acknowledged to herself, that Tamara looked more like her dad than Ann. She had been blessed with his facial features; high cheek bones, wide shapely lips, dimples and beautiful straight teeth. She had healthy, thick curly hair like his that she usually wore in a natural afro style, She had long legs and a narrow waist also like him, but she had Ann's wide hips and pointed chin. Yes, Ann thought, Tamara had been blessed with good genes as had her husband. He was a good looking man, who possessed physical features that had contributed to his tremendous vanity and which had appealed to the opposite sex so passionately, to the point that their attraction to him bordered on idolatry. Ann had initially been swipe away by his appearance also and for a long time had not allowed herself to ponder the obvious flaws of the man. Their romance had been dazzling in the beginning with spontaneous gestures by Jack to impress her like paying for ice skating lessons for the both of them, take her to see her favorite singing groups, the Stylistics and the bluenotes. Things might have frizzled out eventually, she thought, but she had to admit, some good came out of the relationship. Now she looked at Tamara and said,

"Honey if you want to write about your dad and me, go ahead, She paused then continued,

"We were happy in the beginning and we both would have to agree that conceiving you was a blessing from God". She smiled at Tamara.

"For that accomplishment, all the negative occurrences that happened later can be forgiven. Your dad despite his self-absorption, worshipped you and was quite the attentive father, and you were his adoring daughter. He was your hero," Ann laughed as she remembered the good times.

"He might not do all the things he should to be a responsible father; like keeping current with his child support but the man isn't all bad I have to admit", Ann conceded.

Leaning forward, placing her elbows on the table and cradling her face in her hands, Ann reminisced about Jack and her first encounter.

"My friend set up a blind, double date for her boyfriend and herself and invited me along as the date for your father. I was immediately impressed by your father. He was tall, broad shouldered, dark and handsome", Ann remembered.

"I was shy in his presence and hardly said a word during that first meeting, while he rattled on non-stop about himself. That should have told me something about what to expect from the man", Ann laughed, then went on,

"He was a basketball player at his high school and was exorbitant in his enthusiasm for the sport", Ann continued with a smile on her face. "Learnt more about the game of basket ball in those few hours listening to your dad than I had ever known previously".

Tamara laughed lightly as she listened to her mom. She hadn't expected this playful disclosure by her mother; she could quite clearly visualize the over confident, boastful young teen male her father had once been and the naive, captivated young teenage girl her mother had been during that first date. Listening, Tamara contemplated how she would later record in her journal, these memories of her mother. At that moment, Tamara's eyes glanced at the kitchen clock and she realized that if she didn't hurry, she would be late in meeting her friend Ginny, so that they could go together to their dance class. Ginny Thomson was Tamara's best friend since they were classmates during fifth grade. The girls had common interests and soon became fast friends and often slept over at each other's home. Ginny had a dachshund puppy that Tamara loved to play with, further sealing the girls friendship. On sleepovers, Ginny's mother would let the girls eat their dinner on T.V. dinner trays in Ginny's room while they watched Television as Rascel, the puppy, sat close by, begging for scraps.

Today, Tamara and Ginny had their weekly dance class that took place on Saturday. Telling her mother she would continue their discussion later, Tamara gathered her dance paraphernalia and quickly rushed from the apartment.

"It is so much better to die quickly after your soulmate has died, than to live on for many endless, lonely years by yourself, like her", Ginny said, tilting her head in the direction of a homeless woman named Sarah who the girls often saw on their way to dance class.

"You're talking foolishly", Tamara said. "There is a whole world of experiences and blessings to live for after a tragedy of any kind".

On this cool, grey Autumn day, Sarah sat propped up against a smooth, granite wall between the entrance to the Jay Street Metrotech Subway Station, in downtown Brooklyn and the heavily trafficked Citi Bank building. Besides her, piled in disarray, were various soiled, stained packages of Sarah's limited possessions. Tamara and Ginny had adopted Sarah as "their homeless lady" after encountering her during late June for the first time when they had started their dance class at Nzema Ethnic Cultural Center. She wore, at that time, a beige colored dress whose shape or cut you couldn't quite bring to remembrance no matter how hard you tried. They had seen her in almost identical, plain beige outfits ever since. Usually rumbled knee length socks or tights were worn underneath her dress. On her feet were worn, but solid looking black oxfords. On cool days she wore a loose fitting sweater or a torn black jacket. Tamara knew that she had to have worn other colors other than beige, but that was the only color Tamara could remember seeing her in. These attires were draped over what appeared to be a short lithe frame that still hinted at the dancer she once was. For the last couple of months Tamara and Ginny had played detectives trying to find out the history of Sarah. On their first sighting of her, they were struck by the soft, quiet gentle look of this homeless person. Her mouth always seemed to have a little hesitant smile on it that nevertheless lighted up her whole face with the angelic radiance of paintings done by the great master artists. When you looked into her eyes you perceived her whole character. You knew, without having been told, that she was one of those rare, truly gentle spirits who asked for nothing but had given everything early on in her life. All she had left now was this quiet soul still not asking for anything but no longer having anything to give. All this you could discover about her in just seconds from glancing into her huge lugubrious hazel green eyes. From their many inquiries, Tamara and Ginny found out that Sarah was Irish (although her weather beaten olive tone skin suggested Italian ancestry instead) and she didn't seem to have any family around as far as anyone knew. There were rumors of her once having a husband, who died at an early age, and a little son who had vanished one day, never to be seen again. Someone said that Sarah had traveled extensively as a young dancer with a ballet dance troupe of some renown in Europe during the Sixties.

Tamara and Ginny had never heard her speak. Occasionally they would see her lifting her arms and pointing her toes as she would slowly and gracefully turn; doing a fancy ballerina spin. Her posture would be regal as she arched her back and her face would slip into a remotely haunted contour, suggesting she was seeing some landscape only she could see. Wherever she was in time and place, she seem bathed in utter peacefulness and you could look at her knowing that unless your mind leaped into a similar madness, you would never capture or experience such complete serenity. After a few minutes she would abruptly revert to her usual look of bewildering frightfulness; her existence a question even to herself. Seeing this happen would give the girls a knotty feeling in the pit of their stomach. As they passed her today, she sat quietly rummaging through her belongings. Tamara and Ginny hurried past and entered the train station where they managed to board their train on time.

Arriving at their destination, a few stops later they raced up the stairs from the lower platform and headed to the exit. Outside, they puffed hot breaths into the cool, late morning air as they sprinted the short distance to Nzema's Ethnic Cultural Center. The center was located in the Boreum Hill section of Brooklyn, inside an elegant brick building. The exterior was similar to the neighboring buildings in the area. It was somewhat austere in appearance and dated to the early 1800's. Inside it was quite a contrast; large rooms with high ceilings, decorate with beautiful plaster ornamentations. The floors were solid rich hardwood. Elaborate door knobs and stained glass windows decorated the rooms. On the first level of the building, on one side of the entrance hall, was a large room that was created by knocking down the wall separating two former large rooms, forming one tall expanded area which served as the dance studio. Long windows along the front of the room, let in vast amounts of sunlight and when the drapes in the windows were pulled back, pedestrians walking by outside, could see into the studio, and often the music and dancing inside would attract a large number of curious onlookers.

The second floor of the building was where music lessons were given. On the 3rdfloor was where Nzema and her husband lived and was closed off from the students. Outside in the back of the house was an impressive garden of flowering plants along the edges and front. Towards the back was an area sectioned off that contained various vegetables and fruits. This garden had been planted with dedicated thoughtfulness by Nzema and her husband, who were both avid gardeners.

Reaching the center, Tamara pressed the buzzer and waited with Ginny to be buzzed in. Instead, Nzema, a tall impressive lanky Afro-American woman in her 40's with an aristocratic bearing, opened the door. She gave Tamara and Ginny a severe looking over.

"All right, ladies, I'm not going to ask you why you're late. I'm not a den mother, but please try to make it here on time in the future. Come in and change so you can join us". With an impatient look she turned and walked back into the studio where the other members of the class were assembled going through their warm up routines. Tamara and Ginny quickly made their way to the dressing area and put on their leotards, then returned to the front.

Nzema stood in the front of the studio and called the class to attention.

"Today, class, we are going to try something new; we will tell a story by demonstrating it through dance. I want you to visualize that you are back in time, at the start of the Trans-Atlantic slave trade of West Africa. You will imagine that you are captured and sold into slavery. Picture yourself in your village the day you are captured, see yourselves being shackled and beaten as you are brought to the slave ships. Try to enact all the fury and fear you might experience. Then see the voyage on a rough sea, traveling to a distant land", Nzema's eyes swept over her students and then she continued. "You and a multitude of other slaves are traveling under horrendous and squalid conditions. No sanitary provisions, your human wastes excreted where you lay shackled together", Nzema's eyes pierced into all the students' as she talked.

"I want you to hear the clanking and rattling of the chains; feel their cold, hard weight on your skin. Hear the whips whooping through the air. Feel them as they land on you, cutting huge welts on your flesh. Smell the stink in the air from the rotting wood planks and feces.

Nzema paused, allowing the students to start their mental journey to the past. She walked over to the entertainment wall unit and inserted an African Folk singer's music into the CD player. The music started slowly and softly; drums and flutes with other percussion instruments playing. The voice of the singers could barely be heard in the background soon their rhythmic chanting grew in volume and intensity.

Nzema moved down the length of the studio; demonstrating some of the dance steps she had taught the class, beckoned the students to use them in interpreting her storyline.

"Besides you lay slaves, some who are moaning and heaving with the tossing of the ship. Everyone is bound and unable to maneuver their arms and legs into any comfortable position. The pain of your lack of freedom of movement and the long hours of being cramped in tightly with the other slaves overwhelms you. Some of you wish to die, but others stubbornly refuse to lose your mind".

Soon, most of the students had transported themselves into these vivid imagined scences created by Nzema's words and were acting them out in dance steps. Tamara found herself deeply affected and her mind was in a frenzy by the time Nzema told the class to walk up the imaginary steps from within the hull of the ship, leading to the deck where they were to be exercised and allowed to dance. At this point, lost in her created dance, Tamara threw herself at one of her imaginary captors, and let out a piercing scream that startles the other students. They all stopped their dancing and watched in amazement as Tamara did a tumble sauce and flipped over and over across the dance floor as she enacted wrestling with her captors and in a suicidal plunge, hauled herself and her captor overboard, in traumatic climax. By now even Nzema had stopped and mesmerized, stared at Tamara who now laid prone on the dance floor in exhaustion. Nzema's mouth was opened in shock and she clapped her hands in applause. It turned out she loved Tamara's creation.

On her way home, Tamara was bursting with excitement and deep pleasure from the praises Nzema had given her. She found her mind drifting and not concentrating as Ginny tried to engage her in conversation. Eventually the girls arrived back in their neighborhood. They parted from each other as they reached Ginny' block, promising to phone each other later. Tamara continued along, her every step forward energized by the expressed admiration and praise of her dance class. Arriving at her building still full of energy, she pushed opened the front door and immediately felt a bump and then heard a scream of pain coming from the other side of the opened door. Startled by the noise, Tamara cautiously pushed the door all the way open. Standing on the other side of the entrance, rubbing his nose, was a dark hispanic young man that Tamara guessed was a few years older than herself. She also noticed that he was handsome with an expression of intense pain on his face. Quickly Tamara stuttered.

"Oh, I am so sorry. I didn't mean to hit you. Are you alright?"

The young man looked at her and smiled, in spite of his obvious pain."

"Yes, don't worry, I'm alright, apology accepted." He grinned broadly.

"Hi, my name is Manny", he said still grinning.

Still a little embarrassed by her action, Tamara returned his greeting.

"And my name is Tamara. Are you sure you're alright? You looked like you were in a lot of pain a moment ago".

"Oh, don't worry. My nose is not broken, just a little bruised", Manny laughed.

"But it is okay. I got a chance to meet you, so it's all good".

Tamara found herself pleased by his remark and she wondered if she was smiling goofily like an impressionable young girl. She abruptly tried to put a serious expression on her face, she asked him if he was just visiting or if he was a new tenant in the building, explaining she was happy to meet him.

"I've just come from knocking on my friend Raul's door but it seems that he is not home", Manny explained.

"He lives on the second floor, do you know him?"

"Sure, he's a great guy. Everyone here knows him", Tamara acknowledged. Raul was her blind sixty year old neighbor who lived below her. She and Ann frequently spoke to him and enjoyed their conversations with him. They thought he exemplified the image of a caring father figure; a good strong man, always supportive and easy to talk to.

"I believe he might be at his job over at the neighborhood community center", Tamara reflected as she tried to remember the days Raul usually worked at the Genesis Awakement Center. He only worked part time, she believed he had told her and Ann. As Tamara was trying to recall this information, Manny watched her with a broad grin of amusement as if he was taking an assessment of her; who she was for some purpose only he knew. Tamara suddenly became aware of his big grin of delight and a mix of self entertainment, at her expense, and the elements of an intricate game.

"Well, I hope you find him there. I am sure he should be there now", she hurriedly said. "I have to go. It was nice meeting you. Tell Raul, that I said 'hello', if you see him tonight. Good-bye". She turned quickly and rushed up the stairs, hardly hearing Manny's words of "Good-bye, I hope I see you again".

MANNY

Manny quickly descended the stairs of the Marcy Avenue Train Station and exited onto Broadway, his eyes racing up and down the avenue, as he thought about his encounter with the young teenage girl named Tamara, who he had meet earlier in the day. The early evening shadows hung on the edges of storefronts, trying to stay as long as possible before being replaced by the black of night. Manny's eyes scanned the avenue, watching the activities of the other pedestrians. Broadway always seem to draw like a magnet an assortment of people; crowds of shoppers trying to purchase necessary items from the neighborhood stores; mothers with strollers pushing their babies; exhausted men and women on their way home from work; and teeming array of other people coming and going to some destination. Tonight was no different. The evening air was uncomfortably chilly and Manny zipped his blue parka jacket up to his chin and adjusted his back sack containing his gym clothes and stuffing his hands into his pockets, he maneuvered his way through the crowd. He passed Huang's Fish and Chip Restaurant, where fresh fish was sold on one side of the store and fried fish and french fries were served to customers at a long, pink enamel counter that stretched down almost the length of the store, on the opposite side of the store. Manny looked into the window of the store and waved to Chin Huang's wife Lin, who was standing near the cash register, ringing up a customer's bill. She looked over and saw Manny at the window. He waved at her and she returned his wave, giving him one of her small accommodating smiles.

Manny reached the corner and turned down Hilberry Street and walked towards the entrance of the large, burnt red brick building in the middle of the block. This building was the Williamsburg Community Health and Restoration Center, but the community residents had recently fought to renamed it The Genesis Awakement Center. Some people still called it by it's old name but most of the young people referred to it by its new name. The building like most of the other buildings in the area had been built in the early 1900's and could now stand to have some restorations to it's facade which had some loose bricks along the top, held by crumbling mortar and there was peeling paint on the front door and along the trim around the windows and roof line.

The inside though, was always brightly lit and rich, warm toned wood paneling running along the hallways and freshly painted walls in each room created an almost regal and comforting atmosphere.

Manny briskly made his way up the stairs and into the building. Inside he greeted some of the familiar guys from his group session and other guys who he saw regularly while working out in the gym. A few people he did not know stood in groups or were walking through the lobby on their way to or from classes, Manny strolled towards the gym. Standing outside the gym door was Raul, the counselor he had been looking for earlier. Raul was the part time counselor for his group therapy sessions at the center. There were other support staff for the center; some working full time or like Raul, part time, but Raul was considered the friendliest and most dedicated, and his blindness didn't hinder him in doing his job. He didn't pull any tricks with the clients; he was straight forward in his approach when dealing with others and most of the guys in the group thought well of him and found that they could open up to him without feeling that he would negatively judge them. Manny had developed a fondness for the older man that surprised and pleased him. He felt a kinship towards Raul that he didn't feel with anybody else, including his family.

Raul was wearing dark, shaded glasses and khaki pants below a hooded black jacket. His walking cane held lightly in his right hand, at his side. When Manny got within a few feet of Raul he called out a greeting to him with affection. The older man raised his head and with a big grin, said,

"Que pasa, Manny. Que lo que Esta pasando?"

Manny reached Raul and playfully jabbing at the space in front of Raul's face, making whooping sounds imitating the landing of punches to the flesh.

Hi Raul, I'm fine and how's it going with you? Are you ready to defend yourself?" Manny joked as he bounced back and forth on the balls of his feet in imitation of a seasoned prize fighter, throwing intricate fake punches that were in synch with his feet work.

"Kid, don't you know better than to mess with this old Lion? Blind or not I can take you down with one blow to that smart alecky head of yours", Raul's face came alive with the pretend threat. Both men, young and old, grabbed each other in a strong father/son embrace.

"Hey kid, listen, all joking aside, there's something I want to discuss with you" The expression on Raul's face became serious and he released Manny.

"Let's step outside and talk in the backyard", Raul said.

"Sure, anything you want", Manny replied with a slight lift of his eyebrows. Bending down he picked up his back sack, which he had dropped on the floor, and followed Raul out the rear exit door".

As the door closed behind them, Manny looked expectantly at Raul and wondered what he wanted to discuss. Raul's face was ambiguous. It was all starts and no finish; going from a questioning expression, with mouth agape one minute then shut tight the next, an eyebrow raising in concern.

"What is it Raul, what's causing you to hesitate?" Manny questioned.

Drawing in the cold night air, Raul swallowed and responded,

"It's just about what someone told me yesterday. He said he had seen you on Hicks and Juliep, in a vacant lot last week, throwing a ball against a wall."

"Okay, what about it?" Manny said with slight confusion.

"Well, this guy said he was impressed with your pitching and that you have a powerful arm and he would bet his whole paycheck that you were Major League material just like your brother".

While Raul was talking, Manny's eyes followed two women coming up the street. One was pushing a baby carriage in front of her while carrying on an animated conversation with the other woman while a little boy walked some distance behind them. While still watching the approaching women and children, Manny said.

"No way, I just fool around some, trying to get the arm stronger. When I'm feeling in the mood, I go over to the lot to practice pitching and catching. Nothing to it really. The arm is alright I guess but your informant doesn't have good vision if he thinks I'm Major League material.

Just then the two women and children passed by Manny and Raul. The little boy seem even farther behind the women and baby. His face was tear stained and he was whimpering while calling out,

"Momma, momma". Neither women seem to hear him and continue talking to each other, filling the night air with their laughter.

Manny turned letting the cold night air blow into his face, lifting the hair away from his forehead. A quietness seem to come over his whole body and he stared intensively at the passing women.

Raul, not being able to see Manny's expression, somehow sensed, with the sagacity that some individuals possess, the sudden change in Manny's mood. Raul quietly listened to the nuances in vocal tones of Manny's words and quickly read these signals.

"Well I don't want to press the issue, just wondered if you are that good and if you are, why haven't you been out trying out for one of the pro teams. Surely your brother Fernando could get his team to look you over", Raul said casually.

Manny's glance swept down the length of the yard and his eye focused on some unseen object across the street. Raul's inquiry was left unanswered, floating on a barrier of ambiguousness. Raul reached down into his pant's pocket and brought out a pack of Newports cigarettes and with steady hands, lit one for himself then handed the pack to Manny. Manny withdrew a cigarette and mumbled. "Thanks". He lit the tip and inhaled slowly.

"Listen, Manny, I'm not trying to pry. If I'm stepping on an issue you would rather not discuss I apologize. I just felt maybe you might want to talk", Raul leaned in closer to Manny.

"We've known each other for a few months now and it's just that sometimes when I listen to you in the group sessions I get the impression that there is something on your mind that you want to talk about that you haven't been able to verbalize. Something that you haven't shared with anyone. I'm not a social worker or psych doctor like some of the other staff here at the center. I'm only a person who had to do some sorting out myself to get off the downward destination my life was taking. But I'm a good listener and have listened to quite a few stories over the years" He paused, then continued.

"You've told me your dad is on the road a lot, driving a truck for his job. What about your Mom?" Do you and her talk things over?"

Manny's mouth tightened into a slight grimace and his soul stepped away from him. He watched himself, calmly observing the confusion and loneliness that had been his companion since he was a little boy; staying as if an invitation had been extended. The tear stained face of the little boy, who had passed by a few moments ago, leaped into his mind. He thought of his mother's cold indifference this morning when he had greeted her, as he prepared to get ready for work. She was sitting in the kitchen reading the morning newspaper like she did every morning as far back as he could recall. And like most mornings, she didn't even look up as she mumbled "Buenos dias, Manny". With a sudden heave of his shoulder, Manny left that memory and glanced at his friend.

In a voice out of childhood, Manny managed to whisper.

"Leave her out of this conversation. My mother and I don't communicate. Never have, the connection was never there". Raul's ears pickled with the sadness that he heard in Manny's voice. Cautiously he chose his words carefully and said gently.

"Some hurts run deep don't they son?" He placed his hands on Manny's shoulder.

As if a long awaited signal had been given, Manny exhaled deeply and a choking moan tumbled out of his mouth and he trembled slightly. Instinctively Raul grabbed Manny and pulled him close. Manny's reserve was unshackled and a profound anguish washed over him and competed with the sudden rage he felt. He perceived a weakness in his legs from the mixed emotions overtaking him and he stumbled forward. Raul's arms tighten around him and steadied him in a steel like grip. Ashamed at this momentary weakness, Manny glanced around the court yard with the haunted, enraged look of a trapped, angry animal. Had it not been for Raul's powerful grip, he probably would have smashed his fists into the wall next to them. He shook himself free from Raul and inhaled deeply to clear his head from the inner turmoil building up inside it. Sensing that he was calmer now, Manny continued sucking in cold air and steaded himself as he stepped forward and reached for Raul's calloused, aged hands and squeezed them firmly in his own, to show his gratitude for the concern expressed by Raul. He knew he could safely talk now without an outburst.

"Sometimes I rather she didn't look at me, because when she does, it is as if she looks right through me and I think she hates me. I know that's not really true and I don't want to think that way, but her look is so cold and devoid of warmth, I sometimes feel as if she doesn't feel the same about me as she feels about her other children. Fernando, he's her heart. He never could do anything wrong in her opinion". Manny paused and pulling his left arm out of his jacket, he rolled up the sleeve of his sweat shirt and placed Raul's hand on a long scar on his forearm.

"Feel that, that's where my brother cut me while we were playing a game of pirates one day when we were kids. I had found my father's hunting knife in the back of a desk drawer and showed it to Fernando. He grabbed it from me and started pretending it was a sword. Before I could react and move out of the way, wouldn't you know it, I ended up getting cut. Man, there was blood everywhere. It took nineteen stitches to close the wound, but all my mother screamed about, was how it was all my fault for taking my father's knife out of the drawer". Manny stopped momentarily, remembering the incident.

"Fernando didn't get a beating or even disciplined at all. He was truly upset and sorry though. He kept asking me if it hurt and said over and over that he was sorry. He let me take his top bunk bed that night because he knew that was my favorite I got more compassion from my brother than from my mother. She dismissed it as if it was some incidental matter of little importance. She never embraced me or tried to comfort me. Her indifference over the years confused me until I thought I finally figured it out; she was ashamed of me, of my darkness. Her other children were lighter, more like her color. I came into the world and grew darker day by day, even darker than my father. People tell me I look like my father's father. Grandpa was a dark Cuban. Everyone says when they look at me, they see him; a big dark moody man. I've heard this all my life from people and it always seem as if they thought that that was somehow bad."

Manny's eyes were a haunted veil of ambiguity as he searched to express himself.

"Everything I ever did went unnoticed. The good grades I used to get in school, they never were acknowledged. Eventually I just quit bothering. What was the use, if no one ever told you that you had done good. Bringing home a C or a D grade, at least got me some attention. With her screaming you knew you were alive. With Fernando it was always different. Everything he did was a major achievement. If you were praised as much as him, even you, Raul, would have made it into the Major League, in spite of your blindness". Manny snarled in contempt. Compassion and contemplation, both epiphanies, occurred at once to Raul, but he said nothing. He waited for Manny to continue.

"I didn't care what anyone thought of me; I flunked most of my classes, didn't do my homework, wasn't in class half the time. I hung out with other guys whose own priority wasn't school. We smoked marijuana, brought wine and stayed high. I'd come home and scare my little sisters. I felt real bad about that but couldn't seem to stop. It was ugly. My mother had my father talk to me when he was in town. He gave me an ultimation; either shape up or he would bodily throw me out of the apartment. It only worked for the length of time he was there. As soon as he left to go on the road for his cross country job as a truck driver it was back to the same old things. Then one day I found myself knocking on one of my neighbor's door. It was this church going lady and I knew she thought well of me, so there I was asking her to lend me ten dollars. My intentions were to use the money to buy drugs to get high, but I told her my mom was not home and that I needed the money for food. I said I would repay her the next day", Manny said, then pausing for a beat said,

"Raul that lady looked me in the eyes and I could almost hear her thoughts. It was as if she was saying to herself, "he's on drugs", but you could see in her face that she was battling with her decision, whether or not she should give me the money. She didn't want to believe I would use it to buy drugs. She had always encouraged me and whenever we spoke, she was always very friendly", Manny's words sounded as chilly as the night.

"The next day I never showed up to return her money and I didn't see her for two weeks. I encountered her one Sunday morning as I was coming home from an all night High", Manny said. Raul heard his shame.

"Man, she didn't even ask me for the money, she just wanted to know if she could pray for me. She told me that I didn't need to tell her what was going on but whatever it was, God could fix it. We stood right there in the lobby of the building with her holding my hands and praying for me. I went home that day Raul, and threw all the drugs I had in the toilet where they belonged. I really wanted to change. I got myself a job at Flatbush Delicatessen which is downtown and it was there that one of the customers told me about this place".

"I'm glad that person told you about the center Manny", Raul automatically said, nodding his head.

"Yes, I'm glad".

"This place has been wonderful, with all the activities and being able to rap with the other guys in group sessions, meeting you, Raul, and the other counselors has taken away some of the bitterness. I don't feel depressed all the time anymore".

Raul stood there wondering what he could say to Manny. He felt surely he could say something to him that would impact some wisdom if not anything else. Wisdom that would help Manny know that things could be different, were already changing. Everything had a solution, he felt. You just had to find it.

"Manny do you love baseball? Have you ever dreamt that you were standing on the mound at a world series game; your back to the screaming crowd, winding your arm up ready to release that ball that would strike out the opposing team?", Raul inquired gently.

Manny's mouth formed a sly grin as he listened to his old friend.

"Yeah, sure", Manny answered sheepishly.

"I know you have, my friend told me you must have been pitching that ball at ninety-five miles per hour. He said it was the most impressive thing he had seen. Said your catch was good too". Manny's grin got even wider.

"He said if he could pitch like that he wouldn't be in some vacant lot, no, he'd be out front in some baseball field auditioning for one of those baseball scouts who are always searching for new talent. Said he could see himself in one of those baseball farms getting primed for the big times, because with an arm like yours, there would be no way he wouldn't realize his dreams", Raul said.

"Tell your friend I appreciate his praises, but I'm really not that good honestly. Anyway not as good as Fernando", Manny smiled tightly.

"Oh, so you fall into that not good enough mentality. Well your brother may be more talented, gifted and admired than you but is that really important. Isn't it more important that you play the game you love and be the best you can be? Who knows, Manny, its possible that you are just as talented and gifted. If you aren't it doesn't matter. Not everyone who has ever played the game was a Babe Ruth, Jackie Robinson, Joe Di Maggio, Willie Mays or Hank Aaron. It takes teamwork to win a game. Can you be a team player, giving your all for your team. That's all that matters. Giving your gifts, your talents to help your team. Star players are great but you'll never see them win a game single-handedly by themselves", Raul said, warming to his task.

"And your mother, son, she is only a victim like all the rest of us, of the hateful consequences of racism that has misguided and confused many of us; racism that unfortunately has been around since the beginning of time. Some of us realized early that no race is superior, that no physical feature or color of your race makes you any better or worse than the next man. Some of us, never realize that. Those people lead lives at only a fraction of what they could experience; mothers refusing to see grandchildren because they are the product of an union between their child and a person of some other race; missing out on all that love that could be gifted to them; two people never getting to know that they are ideal friends - friends that could form a bond that great literature expounds upon - because they never saw beyond the race of each other, never daring to form a friendship because they were too cowardly to risk the riff of their peers who would frown on such friendship. But being blind Manny, I can't see the difference in other people's appearance, things that are suppose to make us different and I thank God that I can't. He has made me impervious to all of that by my blindness. I might be foolishly lead by the demonic, hateful, stupid influence of Satan, like so many others. I can't see racial differences but I can see character real good and I've seen yours, Manny. No matter how your mother treats you or how the world treats you, God wants you to stand tall and remain strong, not allowing the world to cause you to not strive to be all that God destined you to be. This sad world has taught your mother wrongly (if in truth she feels the way you suspect) it has feed her misinformation, taught her less than the truth. Son, when you go home today, bend down and kiss her on the cheek, tell her you love her and that she is beautiful. Act as if you are her favorite child and if when you do this, she doesn't respond, don't stop, continue to do it until the day she goes to her heavenly rest and when she is gone, you will know that you gave her respect and honor, because she was your mother; and love because like all of us, she deserves that too. Let your love manifest God's agape love that the church talks about. If you do this, I guarantee you, even if you will never know it, you will change her. She might not realize it herself but some small voice within her will tell her that she was wrong. In spite of what her behavior is, you do the correct, moral thing. Let your love teach love through the empowering love of God". Raul said with finality and hugged Manny's shoulder once again.

"Come on son, let's go back inside, where it is warm. Out here, it feels as if ten blizzards have arrived", Raul said, laughing heartedly.

Together, they went inside and Raul thought about all the hurt souls affected by this world's vile host of evil, Satan. He recalled his young neighbor Tamara's poem that she had read to him for his advice. She called it 'We all are Hitler'. He thought of it's words;

WE ALL ARE HITLER

I wonder if Hitler had to start over, would he have faced the future as the original Hitler, kept that name of shame originally given him, that's so hated by the world. Would he have kept that same face so recognizable, face life bravely with his new philosophy. Would he face the many hostile stares at his approach

Would all mankind's judgement, based on his past bother him.

Would his days reflect a new person, based on God's strength.

Would it matter to him, that he had a new outlook but the same original face. Could he surmount the world's opinion of his original self, and boldly declare his new birth in Christ. Would doors fling open in opportunities to this new Hitler, with the same appearance of the original face. Could there be chances given him like every child of God, not hindered by the public's resentment. Can past mistakes, recognized for what they were, widen his capacity to handle his existence with new found strength and mold a future, inspite of the same old face. Would there emerge some desire to hold firm to this new personhood with its still same face. How hard would all the challenges and testing be. To walk among men and still hold that same old face up without shame, but with dignity, like every other beloved child of God. To live this new life he knew he was entitled to. After all, he would now be born again, says the Lord. This is meant to be his right, given by God's promise of salvation. The promise of salvation given by Love. God's infinite agape Love. A love so strong, most can not even fathom its immensity, its eternity etched in the rock that God builds his church. Love with the ability of healing and restoring. Love that gives endlessly, without the needing of repayment, only our obedience of holiness, demonstrated by 'the Son'. Could life promised in abundance, be Hitler's to grasp, holding on to this strength, called Love.

Raul had told Tamara that he loved the poem and thought it had surprisingly a depth of wisdom that he marveled at. Now thinking about it in relation to his talk with Manny, he questioned if she would one day have something of immense importance to say to the world through her writing. She had told him her mother used to write proficiently and often at one time but for some reason unknown to Tamara, had stopped writing. "Hum", Raul thought in contemplation.

TAMAR'S JOURNAL ENTRY, SEPT

Today Ginny and I encountered Sarah, an homeless woman we have seen numerous times on our way to dance class at Nzema's Ethnic Cultural Center, and we thought about all the various stories that we have heard about her from people who knew something about her life. Little by little we have been able to get some idea of her past and how it might have contributed to her present situation; homelessness and mental instability. It is heart breaking and we feel empathy for her and the large community of homeless people we have in New York City and across the country. I think about my dream the other night, about the vision of homeless people gathered around a trash can trying to stay warm. The vision seem to reflect the end result of the era of our world going on a downward path from all the ills of crack, heroin, Aids, rampant unemployment and racial hatred.

The many pieces of Sarah's life bring many questions. She is known to have been a dancer of some renown in Ireland and throughout Europe. The name "Prime Ballerina" was given to her by her adoring fans. Then quite abruptly she married and left Ireland with her new husband. No one knows if she ever danced again. Tamara and I now know she had given birth to a little boy and when he became five his father, Edmond died mysteriously of some illness. It is rumored that he might have been poisoned by a priest he had known as a child back in Ireland. We have heard this priest had been brought before his cardinal to answer charges that Edmond had brought against him when he was here in America. The charges were of sexual abuse. People say it never could be proven, but Sarah was so devastated that she was in a mental fog for months after her husband's death and that during that time, her son mysteriously disappeared, at which point, Sarah never recovered, having blamed herself for her son's disappearance. I hope she eventually will get help. I pray for her daily.

SARAH'S STORY

Sarah hurriedly sponged on talc powder over her face on top of the pancake cream makeup she wore and hoped she wouldn't perspire too much under the brilliant glare of the stage lights tonight. Surrounding her were other dancers also going through the nightly ritual of applying makeup and putting on costumes in preparation for tonight's performance in the Hall of the Mayo Royal Ballet Theater. Tights were eased up legs with meticulous care; skirts and leotards were pulled up over hips as the young dancers of Mayo Royal Ballet playfully joked and exchanged the latest gossip among themselves. The dressing room was charged with an undercurrent of fervent excitement and anticipation of the Ballet they were to perform tonight, Giselle, which was one of the favorites among all the dancers, male and female. Sarah was to dance the part of Giselle, a village maiden. The Ballet was based on the story of beautiful young girls, known as Wilis, who are engaged to be married but because of supernatural powers that intervene, they die before their wedding date. When evening comes they rise from their graves and dance in the light of the moon dressed in their bridal gowns. Their mystic beauty draws in suitors who are forced to dance with them until they drop from exhaustion, and die. Gieselle in the story is romanced by Albrecht, a duke, who leads her to believe he is a peasant. He is already engaged to be married to a prince's daughter and he does not tell Giselle. A jealous gamekeeper, Hilarion, finds out the truth and tells Giselle. In her anguish, Giselle goes insane and then imagining that nothing has happened, rushes to dance with Albrecht. During the dance she becomes frightened and runs to her mother. She falls and Albrecht comes declaring his everlasting love. Giselle forgives him and dies. During the second act of the Ballet, Albrecht comes to visit Giselle's grave and kneels in prayer. Giselle appears and touches him. Together they dance off into the forest. While they are gone, Hilarion comes in mourning to Giselle's grave and is caught in the dance of the Wilis who appear and is forced to dance to his death. When Giselle and Albrecht return the Queen tries to force the same fate on Albrecht. Giselle pleads on behalf of Albrecht. But the Queen will not listen and commands Giselle to dance with Albrecht. Albrecht manages to exhaustingly dance until dawn when he is released from the spell of the Wiles with the approach of daylight. The whole Ballet has expressive, magical dancing where the dancers of the Mayo Royal Ballet Theater take floating leaps, do dazzling spins and brillant pas de deux. Sarah's portrayal of Giselle was always great and her scene of descendance into madness was stupendous. In the dim light the dancer's costumes glittered and the faces of the dancers seemed to effervesce with the anticipation of the performance they would give tonight.

Sarah also felt the excitement of the evening and turning her head she stole a glimpse of herself in the full length mirror that covered the expanse of one wall. Looking down at her legs in admiration of their muscle tone, Sarah pointed her toes. She did not think of herself as beautiful. Her face, she thought, was what most males would consider merely the face of a pretty wholesome woman. She had green eyes that took on a hazel cast in certain lighting. Her hair was naturally wavy and reddish brown. When happy her eyes were gentle and truly the kindest eyes one could imagine. Lost in the joy of her dancing, her true beauty showed in all of its glory. It was not an elaborate beauty that might fade when age touched its perfection. No, it was a simple beauty based more on an inner radiance that if unscarred by life's sometimes harsh treatment, would remain even after wrinkles and grey hairs make their appearances. All this Sarah was unaware of and felt the strength in her looks were her shapely, slender arms and legs. But no matter, it wasn't important to her anyway. Her only true concern was her dancing. And her dancing showed the promise of a talent which would one day be counted amongst the legendary greats of ballet. Her talent combined with the beauty of her graceful body won her the prestigious honor of lead female dancer, an honor hardly ever given to someone so young and of such limited years of training. She had only very recently (compared to the other dancers) begun her formal ballet training thanks to the initiative of the nuns of St Jude. As an unplanned baby of an unmarried young woman belonging to a wealthy Irish family, and a secret black lover, Sarah was brought to the St Jude's orphanage and left in their care. She quickly by the age of two, demonstrated a keen sense of being able to move her little body in time with the beat of music. As she grew older, the games and customary play of childhood did not seem to interest her. She preferred creating new dances which she would perform with great exuberance and sometimes the other children would follow her lead and dance to the delight of the nuns. Her little arms and legs would joyfully move in rhythm to the music played by some of the nuns; like Sister Elizabeth, who played her guitar in the early evening before retiring to her nightly prayers; or Sister Madeline, who played classical tunes and old popular Irish folk songs on the Baldwin piano in the sitting room. As Sarah's talent rapidly unfolded the nuns realized her great potential and enthusiastically looked for a school to teach her ballet. Finally after some individual introductory instructions by a few local teachers, they were able to enroll her, at the age of thirteen, into the famous Mayo Royal Ballet Theater. Her teacher was Olga Tansey who had danced and studied under Mathlilde Kschessinska, one of the great Polish Ballerinas. Olga Tansey was a brilliant teacher, capable of bringing out the best techniques and style of her dancers. Under her guidance, Sarah became a dancer of some renown and was beginning to become known abroad. But unfortunately along with the thrill of achievement, she also felt the baffling sting of resentment from the other dancers of the troupe. Although she showed respect to the other dancers and her behavior towards them was always exemplary, she still induced their wrath, Simple amenities easily given among themselves sometimes were too burdensome or were just overlooked when they should have been applied to Sarah. But in spite of their discontent they found it not an easy task to not marvel at Sarah's every performance. Her love of dancing was evident in the joy in which she skillfully did her grand port de bras, adagios, or her pas de deux.

Tonight Sarah also felt an added excitement. She wondered if her secret admirer was here tonight. For three weeks she had received lavish bouquets of sweet smelling flowers from an unknown admirer. The theater manager, a little man with a bald head and with a youthful face, Mr Bartly James, had brought them backstage, and with a sly grin, presented the flowers to her. Telling her they were delivered from the flower shop and declaring no knowledge of the sender, he would leave her with the flowers that had a white card stuck in them which stated simply "Faithfully, your admirer". At first Sarah had thought Bartley was playing a joke on her and was himself the secret admirer. He was a widower and since the death of his wife a year ago, he would often sit late at night and talk with Sarah. So naturally, even though the talks were only friendly, Sarah now thought that maybe Bartley's interest was more than the want of simple companionship. With embarrassment she sort the aid of some of the other dancers to spy out front to see if there was actually a secret admirer. Two nights ago two of the dancers, Meegan and Nora, finally caught sight of a handsome, anxious looking young man holding flowers in his hands while talking with the manager.

"Stir up, Sarah, and come take a look at your gaming young admirer", Meegan teasingly pulled Sarah to the side stage door to look at the young man. Sarah hesitantly looked out at the audience.

"Isn't he a gallantly handsome man"'" Nora said admiringly. Nervously Sarah searched the crowd and saw a man who automatically sent a quiver racing through her heart. Handsome she thought he was indeed. He sat up front in one of the balcony boxes that directly overlooked the stage; he was talking to Bartley. He had shockingly red thick hair which was brushed smoothly back with a few strands falling down on his forehead. Red bushy eyebrows sat above gentle but melancholy eyes. His mouth was soft, almost feminine. His body was small, well proportional and hard. In front of him leaning against the balcony ledge, the young man had placed his sketching board, papers and coloring pencils. Sarah continued watching as Bartley left him and came downstairs walking to the stage. Upon seeing the young women peering out the side door he approached them and said,

"Good evening misses and what might you be searching for". Looking directly at Sarah with a big grin, Bartley continued,

"It wouldn't be the fine young man above, that you have your eyes on". Bartley beamed like early morning sunlight.

"Oh, may God correct you, Bartley. Leave her alone, hasn't a lonesome girl the right to let her eyes find a pleasing sight to rest themselves on?" Nora said as she walked away with Meegan.

"It's little I care about your teasing, Bartley. But there's going to be torment for you if you don't tell me now what his name is." Sarah said with mock anger.

"Such talking from such a gentle miss", Bartley scolded. "I was just setting my mind on telling you. His name is Edmond Mahon. A fine, young man he is. But God bless him, he doesn't seem to have much money. An artist he says he is. Makes his living with the brushes and colors. A right nice, shy kind of guy. If I was your father I would be thinking right fitting he is to have your hand".

"Go away, Bartley and leave my sight", Sarah softly said.

"YOU hardly know him, only these few days you've seen him"

with a smile on her face, Sarah ran back to the dressing room, her body almost ready to take a buoyant leap.

Tonight Mr. Edmond Mahon sat in his usual box directly under one of the massive chandeliers that lit the theater and pulled out his preliminary sketches of Sarah and the Ballet Troupe that he had been working on. Edmond ignored the other theater patrons who sat in his box; a middle age couple out celebrating some accomplishment of the husband; two young couples who were happily enjoying each other's company and an elderly gentleman with a mirror image of himself, who undoubtedly was his son, sitting at his side. They all watched with great interest, Edmond's concentrated preparations. Totally absorbed in his work, Edmond tuned them out; their stares and chatter becoming backdrop. His thoughts were on Sarah as he looked over his sketches and saw her beautiful face looking back at him.

Below in the pit, the orchestra, in a low tempo, struck up a fast clipped measure as the theater manager stepped onto the stage. He came center stage and welcomed the audience; with an embellishment of words and gestures, he gave an introductory description of the ballet that was to be presented. The audience erupted in applause at his conclusion and after taking a low bow, Bartley quickly exited off the stage. A hush fell as the music's tempo picked up and first act began. Edmond's hands flew over his sketches adding new details recording the magic of the dancers as they moved to the music. The music's own magic mixed with the magic of the Wilis added to the compelling supernatural beauty of the Ballet.

Two hours later Sarah stood waiting in the wing ready for the clue to come back on stage to take her bow with the rest of the cast of dancers. When it was given Sarah stepped out to a thunderous greeting of admiration. Slowly the clapping subsided and running off stage she nearly collided into Bartley.

"Sarah, the young man is setting his mind on meeting you and bade me to say that he desires to talk with you. He says he will ask your pardon if he is a vain man to think you will give him company". Barley said imploringly.

"Oh my grief, no Bartley, I don't have such bravery of heart You mustn't let him come back here. I have no experience of talking to the likes of him. I'd gift you with a warm knit sweater and matching socks at Christmas if you see that my passage home be free from having to speak to him. Will you talk with him for a while so that I can leave tonight without him seeing me? Oh, I'd be frighten if he should", putting her hands to her mouth, Sarah let out a little sharp cry. Running back to the dressing room, she quickly gathered her things and peeked out the stage door to watch for an opportune moment when Bartley would have the young man's full attention. She would then make her escape.

"My thousand regrets to you son, but Sarah has already left. But come let us sit and discuss a thing or two", Bartly coaxed Edmond.

"You're not from this area are you?"

"No, I'm from further up north of here. Small hillside town called Rose de Rescht", said Edmond. "I've come here to teach painting. I have a few students. One brought me along with him one night so that I could see for myself the fine dancing to be viewed here. So I came and saw that he was not making a brag.

And Sarah's the best. I've never seen the likes of her and that's the truth", said Edmond with rapture.

"But tell me then, will you soon be going home to some girl back home?"

"No, there is no one. But it is Sarah I want to be seeking after, now that I've seen her". Edmond turned toward the stage at that moment and caught sight of Sarah's feet and skirt below the screen that blocked the musicians in the pit from the audience

"Leave my sight, glory to God. You've lied to me. Sarah's not gone from here. There she is passing below". Angrily Edmond pushed Bartley aside and hurriedly ran downstairs. He rushed after the fleeting figure and reached her just as she was about to go through the front door. Sarah's back was facing him and he called out in anguish.

"Sarah, don't leave. I know that we belong together, it's our destiny. Please trust me. Give me a chance to show you. There's so much I want to share with you". He grabbed Sarah's arm, stopping her from leaving the building. She turned and faced him. Edmond stared intensely at Sarah and pleaded with her to listen to him. He gently touched her face and said,

"I want you to share beautiful mornings bathed in sunlight and vibrant sunset colors with me. When I look at you dancing it's as if it's many years I've known you. When you dance I see your soul and it's as if I'm recognizing you as if from a past memory. It's a remembrance so almighty powerful I was afraid at first because I couldn't put a name to it".

Sarah slowly lowered her head, closing her eyes.

"Look at me, Sarah", Edmond said. She looked up at him,

almost in a frighten manner. She was trembling and he lowered his hand from her face and touched her shoulders. She shuddered and slumped into him.

"I will not hurt you, you can trust me", Edmond gently whispered.

"Somehow I know you won't, at least I'm thinking it isn't your intention to cause me grief, Mister Edmond", Sarah said weakly.

Taking her hand he guided her outside to the little pub across the street from the theater and they sat over dinner and beer to talk. She told him about the nuns of St. Jude. He told her about his days as an alter boy at St. Benedict Church. She told him about Sister Elizabeth and Sister Madeline. He didn't tell her about Father Reilly. Sarah told him of her joy of being part of the Mayo Royal Ballet, about her kind benefactress Olga Tansey, who taught her and gave her a place to live. Edmond told her about his love of painting and his many travels. The evening slowly passed as they continued to get to know each other. Finally Edmond walked Sarah home.

After that first night they meet every night after Sarah's performance. They came here to Finnegin's Pub and Eatery. In two months they were married and Sarah moved in with him. The night they were married Edmond told Sarah about Father Reilly. This night they talked long into the early morning and also cried. Edmond trembled from his shame and grief. Again he felt the persistent terrifying agony and fury. He remembered the large rough hands on his small hands; later exploring elsewhere. He once again could hear the deep voice that whispered, "You are so beautiful Edmond", with renewed shame. With tears filling his eyes he told Sarah about his suppressed feelings that had caused him to lose himself in his art. When he was finished he was weak from the emotional release and with Sarah's gentle urgings, gave himself permission to heal.

Later Sarah led him to the bed where cool cotton sheets formed a smooth haven for his tired body. Slowly they undressed and laid next to each other. Sarah looked at him; his skin so smooth and pale, seemed to be washed in gleaming silver luminous rain drops as the moonlight coming in from the open window splattered over it. His eyes were now closed and the muscles in his body all appeared to be pulled taunt as if they were about to jump at the slightest provocation. Lovingly Sarah marveled at his masculine beauty. She slowly swung her body over his then eased herself on top of him. Her hands now moved over his body threading his tight muscles as her breath floated over his face whispering words of her love for him. His eyes opened. She kissed his lips and he embraced her with passion. Warm sensations flooded every inch of their bodies and Edmon moaned as Sarah reached under her stomach and stroked him gently. Her breasts flattened against his chest in a delicious sensation of velvet softness against his hardened muscles. Languishly her hands moved over his body as she caressed him steadily until his body was released from its physical pain and seemed to float on a flowing wave.

Gently and lovingly they shared the ecstasy of intense passion that their love for each other inflamed. Sarah's hands moved over Edmond's body, threading his tight muscles, she quivered as her hands felt the hardness of his abdomen (so different from the softness of hers). She felt the rush of blood to her vagina and softly gasped as pulsing pressure built in the area as Edmond pushed his manhood into her womanhood. The intensity of the rhythmic sensation pulsing in the two lovers built, then the climactic release for both of them seem to go on forever; wave after wave of pleasure. Edmond bent down and lashed onto one of her nipples and greedily started sucking. His mouth moved from her breast and kissed it's way up her shoulder, wandered over her neck and hovered over her soft lips.

"Oh Sarah you are so beautiful", his words caressed her warmly.

"I love you, will always love you".

"Say it again Edmond. I want to hear you love me with your voice".

"I love you, will always love you. To think, tomorrow and tomorrow after I will wake up and you will be beside me to comfort me. Oh how God has blessed me. I was so alone without you, Sarah. You make me feel so alive. Before I never realized how alone I was".

"Me too Edmond, my world was filled with my dancing but now I'm feeling what it is to share joy."

Edmond put one hand between her legs and massaged her. Parting her flesh with his fingers, he entered her. Low moans rose up into Sarah's throat as warmth flooded her pelvis. Sarah's moans increased Edmond's excitement and blood rushed through his body again. Quickly he entered her pumping long and hard as her inner hand met each thrust and squeezed him in return until time exploded in mutual involuntary pulsations in their bodies and stretched into infinity.

Spent, Edmond lowered his head to Sarah's chest and again

grabbed a nipple. Curled up beside her, he continued sucking until he drifted off into sleep with her nipple still in his mouth. The room enveloped them in darkness as they held onto each other until Edmond loosened his arms as exhausted, sleep inevitability pulled him into its dark and silent sphere. Gently as not to disturb him, Sarah reached over and pulled the covers over them and caressed his head as it laid against her breast.

TAMARA'S JOURNAL ENTRY

Today I spoke to that pretty Black young mother, Nettie, who lives with her mother on the top floor in my building. She was out of breath trying to manage getting all of her four children and the packages of food she carried up the stairs, to get to their apartment. It looked like an impossible feat, but somehow she accomplished it. She is divorced from her children's father and recently came here to Brooklyn to live with her mother, Louise. No one has seen her dating and figure she is like many divorced women; hesitant about bringing a man around her children. My mother also has not ventured out into the dating world either. She told me she is quite content with her life as it is. Truthfully, I am hoping her and dad reconcile and get back together again; that is if Dad will do some growing up and change. I know not all black families are splintered like my family and Nettie's, but it seems that quite a lot are. This is probably due to the many stresses that is placed upon the Black family; lack of necessary gainful employment as a result of unequal opportunities for the black person; lack of decent affordable housing for minorities - in spite of the increase in economic success of a few Blacks, too many are at or below the poverty line; thereby quite unable to afford the cost of luxury priced housing that is available in many communities; and the burden of racism that still prevails in society. These kinds of stresses has to influence the way blacks interact with each other - sometimes blaming their hardships on their partners, themselves as well as their oppressors.

NETTIE

The honking of a horn behind her, startled Nettie Morgan awake from her blissful few seconds of sleep in her Ford Taurus at the intersection of Madison Avenue and East 34th Street. She surmised that if a police officer had seen her asleep at the wheel of her car, he would think she was a Black woman high on drugs, as too many police seem to think about Blacks; in her opinion. Alert now, she realized that the traffic in front of her had advanced and she quickly drove her car across the intersection. With an involuntary sigh, Nettie hoped the sleep deprivation she had been experiencing the past two days wouldn't be the controlling factor in her work performance today. Angrily she considered why it was that she hadn't been able to get any restful sleep recently. She sighed again. Her conversation with her ex-husband, Ken, last week was the aggravating cause. One call from the man could shatter her equilibrium. He was making demands to visit their children, yet refusing to tell her when he would send the rest of her belongings that she had not been able to take with her when she left him.

It was 7:40 AM and the air was chilly with the promise of another below normal temperature day. The streets were bumper to bumper, dued to rush hour traffic and the burden of outer towners and international travelers who were coming into the city for the upcoming United Nations Day celebration which was to take place on October 24th. At this molasses pace, Nettie mused, she would not reach the Office of the Chief Medical Examiner of New York City, at her customary 7:45 AM time. Arriving a few minutes early, before the start of the Eight AM shift, was part of her morning routine. She was a newly hired medical examiner assistant and had only been on the job for a mere seven months. Prior to coming to Brooklyn, with her four children to live with her mother, she had been totally contented working at the IBM plant in the rural outskirts of Poughkeepsie, New York, until the desolation and end of her marriage of seven years and the remarriage of her ex-husband to his co-worker, Dr.Ivy Stone. In the early months prior to the breakup, Ken's metamorphosis into a distracted, inattentive mate had bewildered her. Then came the night he had admitted his affair and love for Dr. Stone. The revelation explained the lonely nights she had fretted while waiting for him to come home. Now she had been hit with the ugly truth that he had lied when he had told her that he had been researching treatment protocols and updating his patients' files. She had accepted the lies and had not questioned him because she would also on occasion spend long hours finishing her work at her job. There had been so many changes after the breakup, causing her to feel unnerved most of the time. Her children couldn't comprehend all the changes to their young lives and felt as betrayed as their mother. But children can be forgiving; and had gradually accepted Ivy as their Stepmother but Nettie had found out that she could not be as forgiving and had struggled with severe depression and anger and resentment. Then when she felt that she'd reach her limit, and no longer wanted to wade in victim hood, she applied for the job at the OCME in New York in order to get as far away from her ex-husband and his new wife. Thankfully the move had turned out to be a positive decision. She moved in with her recently widowed mother who had a great reasonably priced Condo apartment in Brooklyn. It was near a lovely park which allowed her and her children to ride their bike along the bike trails of the park on the weekends. The location of the Condo placed the family in close proximity to the Brooklyn Museum, decent restaurants and major subway lines. With time, the vibrant pulse of the City, and her new job, was instrumental in helping her move past her hurt and emotional pain. The new job, as an assistant to the Medical Examiner, with all its challenges, was grueling work and she had decided, after the urgings of her mother, to return to school and work towards becoming a medical examiner. Her mother had always encouraged her to strive for excellence and to fight to overcome the barriers that society had forced on Blacks.

Nettie was pleased to see that the traffic was moving faster now and within ten minutes she arrived at her job and drove into her usual parking space. As Nettie emerged from her car, she was surprised to see Detective Greg Clarkson from the local precinct hurrying towards her. Nettie had meet him the first week she had started working at the OCME. Nettie watched his approach, secretly admiring (in spite of herself) his caramel tan powerful arms bulging from the sleeves of his short sleeves uniform shirt and wondered why he didn't have his jacket on.

Probably intentionally wants to show-off his beautiful muscles, Nettie smirked. He looked like he'd just stepped out of the pages of GQ Magazine.

Nettie smiled inwardly, she thought he looked like an eager little boy, who had just learnt that Christmas had been extended for a whole year. She wondered if today would be the day he finally got up enough nerves to ask her out on a date.

"Good Morning, Nettie", Greg called out to her.

"Good morning Detective Clarkson. Why are you here so early? Nettie questioned.

"I've been up all night", Greg whined, looking somewhat fatigued.

"There was a five alarmed fire a few blocks from here that raged all night long. There have been a few suspicious fires in the city that's causing a major investigation. My precinct was called to join in the search for clues in this neighborhood. I was just coming from the adjunct police office here at the OCME and saw you pull up. I'm going home to get some sleep, but I was wondering if I could come by later, when you get off, to take you out to dinner?" Greg said, the words tumbling out rapidly; as if he was trying to say them before he lost his nerve, scared that Nettie would reject his attempt to further their relationship. Nettie smiled with satisfaction at Greg's invitation that he had finally been able to utter.

"I think I would love that, detective Clarkson", Nettie flashed her sexiest, broad smile, that she could convey without displaying how happy she was.

"well great, but you are going to have to call me Greg from

now on, if we are going on a date", Greg muttered, embarrassed to be showing his happiness also.

"Yes Greg" Nettie beamed brightly at him, "Come back at 5:30 pm, I'll be out front waiting for you, See you then"

"Sure, I will be on time, see you later and have a great day…." the words stumbled out quickly as Greg turned to leave. Nettie watched him leave and then reflected " I have a date. My first official date in years". A little anxious, fleeting concern tightened her throat then she swallowed a deep breath and tried to relax. With determination she gathered all her belongings and hurried into the building pushing thoughts about tonight out of her mind.

Once inside she entered her office and sat down at her desk to call her mother to let her know she would be late in coming home tonight. She hadn't dated since her arrival back home and she knew her mother would be curious and possibly concern about any man she might be interested in. Her mother had not approved of her ex-husband, Ken and waited until the night before her wedding to express her doubts about him being the right man for Nettie. Nettie had been furious and the next day when she should have been ecstatic about her marriage to Ken, she was distracted all day contemplating her mother's potent warning to her. She vowed to herself when she moved back home, that she would try to be patient with her mother's sometimes intrusive ways.

She placed the call to her mother, telling her about her date and was surprised when her mother hardly seemed to register the fact that Nettie had a date for tonight and absently said she would see to the kids, getting their dinner and seeing them off to bed latter. Nettie hung up the phone and thought about her mother's actions lately. Most days she seem a little down, perhaps retirement was making her feel useless. Nettie made a mental note to herself to try to be more encouraging to her mother; maybe she could try to motivate her to try to join the YMCA or some Senior Center. Her mother had lived a life during her marriage of working hard while trying to raise her two children, Nettie and her brother Bob (who now lived in Mississippi).

Nettie's father had adored her mother and Nettie knew her mother probably was also somewhat depressed by his sudden death a few years ago from lung cancer. He had worked using a lot of chemicals in his two jobs; one as office cleaner, using harsh detergents to strip and polish the floors and his full time job helping mix the different concentrations of fragrances and volatile oils in the production of perfumes at the International House of Fragrances and Flavors. He had loved his wife and children and had showered them with lavish affection; spending what free time he had attending to entertaining his children and wife with hilarious tales of his youth, and treating them to his favorite recipe of Cajun Jambalaya; a stew of rice, red bean, shrimp, sausage and chicken; which he enjoyed cooking and when he wanted to give his wife a break from daily cooking, which he knew she did not have a passion for.

Yes, her mother had a good husband and father for her children. He had brought them a house in Jamaica, Long Island, that he had been very proud of acquiring. When he and Nettie's mother had been empty nesters years later, they had moved into the Condo in Brooklyn.

Nettie told herself that she definitely had to look into checking her mother's emotional health. She got up and walked into the Breakroom where she poured herself a full cup of coffee, then returned to her desk and sat down and started on her work for the day.

LOUISE

Louise hung up the phone and thought about Nettie's date tonight. Finally she was getting back into sharing her life with someone other than Louise or her children. Louise had tried to act unconcerned about the situation, she didn't want to be interfering in any way. And if this new man turned out to be another headache like Ken, Louise wanted Nettie to realize that on her own without being influenced to think that by her mother. Louise secretly hope he would be a good man. Her daughter deserved the best. She had spent so much time with someone who didn't appreciate the wonderful person she was. Louise felt happy about the possibility of happiness for Nettie this time around. Part of Louise's positive mood was the large insurance policy she had acquired recently on herself with Nettie and her grandchildren being the sole beneficiaries. They would not have to rely on anyone's help when Louise died. Louise made sure that Nettie would have enough to finish school and buy a beautiful house for herself and the kids. Yes, things were looking good and yesterday Louise had gone to lunch with Eunice from her church and realized just how blessed she was. Eunice had no known relative alive and had to work at the age of 74 at Walmart and Louise wondered how she managed to always seem so happy. She enjoyed her lunch with Eunice and looked forward to a future lunch with her and two other ladies from the church planned for next week. Yes, things were going well, Louise sighed happily.

TAMARA'S JOURNAL ENTRY

Ginny and I are I guess like any typical teenager, we enjoy having fun. Good, clean not any possibility of messing up your life kind of fun though. The drug scene is not for us. Look, we've both have seen, first hand what drugs can do to you. Both of us have either a family member or a friend who has messed up their lives because of some drug. It hurts to see someone who you know and like, who has a world of potential, turn into someone you fear and mistrust. It hurts even more when the addicted person finally realizes how low they have sunk and you see their despair when they battle to regain what they have lost. Too many never succeed, like my old neighbor Glen. Four days after coming out of a detox center last year, he died from a drug overdose.

Hey, Ginny and I both agree, that's not for us. We consider ourselves Fly, intelligent young Black Sisters with an agenda for success. We look around us and see too many young, Black people getting caught in the media lies; lies that portray us as perpetual party animals, having non-stop sex and living with this "I don't gave a damn" attitude about our future. Look at some of the music videos and the young sisters they show, all wearing tight micro skirts or dresses and skin tight pants shaking their butts into the camera. To us, that's a blatant portrayal of Black women as easy, sexual objects with an inborn desire to just bump-n-grind in tight fitting clothes, exposing their bodies as if they were public domain. It is a relief to know that not everyone is buying into this crap. A person has to have the good sense to realize the value of a good education and the need for political and economic power, especially a Black person. This is what the leaders Malcom X and Martin Luther King tried to teach us and died for. And they weren't talking about economic power by hustling and selling drugs or anything else destructive to your people or helping someone who lives in a million dollar home outside your neighborhood, commit genocide against your people. He or she doesn't care how deteriorated your neighborhood gets; they don't have to live in it. My friend, Kwuame, was telling us that brothers and sisters who are doing this and take the money to start a legitimate business are still wrong. No amount of money justifies helping to destroy even one person, one innocent soul. It doesn't justify the things that drugs cause; prostitution, broken homes, along with racism, it fuels crime. When it comes to drugs and the black or minority neighborhoods, contrary to what seems to be happening now, we all need to become radical. I'm not talking about violence. What I would like to see is radical efforts to seriously tackle our present day ills. I'd like to see people, especially in the black community, fully come together and utilize the power of the vote. It does count. Housing suitable for desent living, has to be improved in poor neighborhoods. My mom heard me and Ginny talking about these subjects the other night and said we were beginning to sound like Kwuame.

KWUAME

Kwuame shook his head in frustration as he searched in his pocket for his Transit Card which he needed for today's excursion down to buy some music CD. Once again, he thought, his friend Nat was late as usual. They were supposed to hit the stores on Fulton Street to see if they could find a CD by his favorite pianist and composer, Thelonious.Monk. He wanted to leave early for today's outing because he anticipated that the search might take some time, Monk's music was extremely difficult to find in stores. Kwuame discovered the artist's work when he had visit his aunt in Rocky Mount, North Carolina two years ago. His aunt was a big fan of Monk and told him that Monk had been born in Rocky Mount in 1917 and she knew some of his relatives. It wasn't hard to realize why his aunt was such a fan, he too was captured by the artist's genius and the uniqueness in his tunes of harmony, melody and rhythm. Along with other legends, Dizzy Gillipsie, Charlie Christian, and Kenny Clarke, he helped create the style of jazz, known as bebop. Kwuame also was hoping to find some gospel music by Thomas A. Dorsey, who is considered the father of gospel music. Kwuame had knew Dorsey had written countless songs and published many. He would distribute single sheets of music to singers at churches, offering them for sale. A lot of the churches were at first resistant to this new form of music, but eventually the enthusiasm for the music grew. Dorsey named it gospel music because he felt it represented the message of the gospel Books, the first five books of the New Testament within the Holy Bible, which is considered the good news of the birth and resurrection of Jesus Christ. He really hoped to be successful in his quest to build on his music collection. There were some other musicians that he would look for today also. His mind counted off the various artists they could search for. At that moment he saw Nat walking towards him with that lopsided swagger of his interpretation of a cool guy's walk. Kwuame again shook his head and laughed.

"Hey, man, cut the show, where you been, man? I've wasted a hour waiting on you", Kwuame complained to his friend.

"Sorry, couldn't be helped. My mom made me do some errands for her before I could leave; you know how hyped up she gets on the weekends when she starts on her chores and demands everyone in the house to march to her demands to get the place cleaned", Nat lamented, in return, and then said,

"Don't worry the stores aren't going anyway. You'll get a chance to spend your money".

Kwuame looked with amusement at his friend and laughed.

"Nat, you can talk all the crap you want, but I know if we were going to look for some movies by your favorite film maker and directer Oscar Micheaux, you would be in more of a rush than I am. Say it ain't so, dude." Kwuame shot back.

"Okay, Okay, you got me", Nat laughed. "But I have to ask, can we stop at Big Al's on our way back? I need to see what's happening with Trudy. She's got an attitude about something and is not answering my calls".

"Nat, what have you been up to now? You know Trudy only acts that way when you are not spending enough time with her, or if you are flirting with some other girl" Kwuame said.

Nat looked sheepishly at Kwuame, acknowledging the truth of his remarks. "I might have paid too much attention to her friend Elaine at the party last week when I meet her. She is cute and I couldn't help myself. You know I love the ladies". Nat grinned.

"Oh man, that's the sin of all sins for females; their boyfriends or husbands, scoping their friends". Kwuame whistled under his breath, He really wondered when his friend would grow up and stop his typical womenizing behavior that caused so much emotional pain for women. He, himself, was no angel, but he tried to be faithful when dating. Right now he was not involved with any young lady but hoped whenever he might become involved in a serious relationship with someone in the future, that he would respect and be concerned with his partner's feelings. His mother constantly explained the importance of a healthy relationship with your mate. His father was a good example for him, and also preached integrity between the sexes to him. He knew Nat didn't have that same reinforcement for positive behavior from his family. His father was a heavy drinker and was abusive to Nat's mother during his drinking bouts and thought nothing of staying out all night drinking with friends or whoring with women.

"Listen my friend, treat your lady as the queen she is and you'll never wonder what's happening with her. Stop the clowning and get serious if you really care for her", Kwuame advised. He clapped Nat on the back and they headed to the train station.

Later, downtown finally, they headed into the first store. The selections on the racks were very limited. There weren't many old recordings or CD's by earlier artists from the past. Discouraged they moved on to the next store, a couple of Blocks away and found the same situation there too. Nat stopped on their way out of the store and turned towards Kwuame.

"Look, Kwuame, you might have to go online to get what you are looking for. There aren't that many stores left that sell music. This area is one of the few that still does and look how hard it is to find what you want".

"Yes, maybe you are right. But let's try a few more before we give up, okay?" Kwuame said.

Nat, sighed and proceeded to follow Kwuame up the block heading toward the next store, reluctantly accompanying his friend on what he considered was a fruitless venture. As they continued Nat looked at Kwuame and asked.

"Hey Kwuame, haven't seen your uncle Khaaliq around recently. How is he? Is he still in the area? I know he was talking about leaving and going to Ohio to start a chapter of "Brothers United" (a coalition of Christain Brothers in faith from different racial groups).

"He is doing fine and is still in the area. Said he hasn't been able to finalize his plans yet", Kwuame said.

Kwuame's uncle, Khaaliq, was a former Black Panther, who was still active in trying to improve the economic and living conditions of Blacks in this country and hoped to start a wider initiative to encourage change. He had preached on the importance of knowing one's history and achievements that unfortunately wasn't fully told for the Black man and woman in this country and elsewhere in the world. Kwuame remembered when his uncle had shared with him and Nat the proud accomplishments of the first African-American aviator, Bessie Coleman, born 1892 in Atlanta, Texas. Uncle Khaaliq told them that Bessie had secured training at the finest school in France, Ecole d'Aviation des Freres Caudron. She came back to America after getting her pilot License and began lecturing at schools and churches. She was an exceptionally skilled pilot and also a beautiful woman. It was her dream to open a flight school for African Americans. But before she was able to make that a reality, she died in a plane crash when she flew with a novice pilot, William Wills, who was at the controls of the plane.

Kwuame and Nat were so impressed with Bessie Coleman's story that they begged Khaaliq to tell them about some of the other Black unsung heroes that he had learned about. Nat, wanting to become a film director, listened attentively to Khaaliq's summation of African American, Oscar Micheaux, born 1884 - 1951, who was born in Cairo, Illinois. Micheaux founded his own publishing company, wrote novels, and then became an influential film maker who sort to portray Blacks in a manner contradictory to how Hollywood was portraying them at the time; as devoted servants or African savages. He wanted to portray Blacks with dignity and respect in non-racist representations and created over thirty-five films. Oscar Micheaux became Nat's conception of the ideal role model for his goals of becoming a Black film director.

"Why don't we head over to Manhatten where the Schomburg

Center for Research in Black Culture is located", Nat said. "You uncle talked a lot about it and I would like to see it"

Kwuame recalled his uncle's intensity when he first told the two of them about the educational and inspiring aspects of this well known landmark in Harlem. He told them the Schomburg Center was formerly the Division of Negro Literature, History and prints, of the New York Public Library. Arthur Schomburg, born 1874 - 1938, was made curator of the center in 1932 and the Center's name was changed to its present day name, after his death in honor of him. Mr. Schomberg, born in San Juan, Puerto Rico, became interested in fellow African Americans' history and amassed an extensive collection of historical documents, texts, and images of African Americans. His goal was to showcase the history of African Americans for the building of pride and inspiration for Blacks. Kwuame thought about Schomberg's devotion to this cause and also reflected on the words of Heavy Weight Boxer Joe Louis Barrow in 1935 regarding what Rev. J.H. Maston had told him, after his defeat of Primo Carnera on June twenty-five. Joe Louis said the Reverend had talked about "God gave certain gifts.....and through my fighting I was to uplift the spirit of my people. I must make the whole world know that Negro people were strong, fair, and decent" Thinking about this, Kwuame turned to his friend and said,

"That is a great idea, but I thought you wanted to go over to Big Al's"

"I think I'll let Trudy calm down some more before seeing her" Nat laughed.

"Well, let's decide after checking out a few more stores"

Kwuame said. They had reached the "Phenomenal House of Blues and Jass and entered through a large glass paneled door with music notes stenciled on it's surface. A little bell clank as the door closed behind them, letting the owner of the store know that customers had entered the store. Walking along the aisles displaying CDs and albums of some of the greats of the Blues genre, Kwuame stopped abruptly and reached out to grab a CD of "Memphis Blues" which was written by William Christoper Handy, the African American credited with being the or one of the fathers of Blues Music. This hit along with Handy's St Louis Blues were said to be the beginning of a brand new phase in music, The Blues. which was inspired by old black spirituals, and working man's songs, and was captivating with its melancholy sound produced by flatted thirds and sevenths.

"Wow, I can't believe they have a copy of Handy's "Memphis Blues", Kwuame said, examing the CD in his hands, handling it like it was a precious piece of gold.

"This could be enough of a find to make this day more than a success", he chuckled. "But let's continue looking around. This may be where we will find some of Monk's music".

Twenty minutes later, after searching in a side rack, along the back wall of the store, they came across a copy of "Thelonious Monk genius of modern music". Kwuame was ecstatic once again. He was immensely pleased that the CD included two versions of his favorite piece "Ruby My Dear; the original and the alternate interpretation. Most people felt the alternate version was more circumspect and Kwuame concurred. He pointed out to Nat that the CD also had the playful, energetic alternative take of "Well you needn't" which was one of Kwuame's favorite pieces of Monk's music.

Nat, yawned and stretched his arms sideways and said,

"Kwuame, look I'm getting tired and hungry from all these hours of walking. We are a block from Sadie's Soul Kitchen, so why don't we head over there and get something to eat?"

"OKay, I know how you get when you are starving for food", Kwuame laughed, and the two walked the short distance to the restaurant.

They went inside and sat at a front booth. When the waitress came to take their orders, Kwuame ordered Buttermilk fried Chicken, blackeyed peas, with collard greens plus cornbread. Nat decided on Red Beans and rice with smoked ham hocks along with a side of Creole Okra with tomatoes. Once the food arrived both teens dug in with relish as if they hadn't eaten in years. With big grins on their faces, they settled back in their seats quite content.

"Man, I am not going to marry a sister unless she can cook like this", Kwuame laughed.

"Trudy can cook, but she tends to get easily distracted and half the time a good dish she has cooked will get burned to a crisp because she has her mind on something else besides watching the food cooking", Nat squealed with laughter recalling some of the ruined meals Trudy had made.

"Yea, I'm sure you caused some of those distractions for her", Kwuame smirked.

"Besides, we are sounding sort of sexist, as if a woman's only value is being a cook, you know a lot of men enjoy cooking for their families. You and I need to be enlighten Black men and get with the times", Kwuame smiled at his friend.

"Come on, Kwuame, I'm a modern guy, but I don't want to be in the kitchen cooking. I know my limitations and if my wife can't cook, we will be in some trouble; we'd be one of the skinniest couples around, you know it man", Nat joked.

TAMARA'S JOURNAL ENTRY

Today upon entering my apartment building, I caught a glance of my neighbor John looking out of his window; I'm not sure that he was actually looking at me or if he just was looking out upon the street in front of the building. He lives on the first floor of the building, this probably was for convenience sake and the need for easy access in and out of the building. He is disable and physically challenged; he also appears to be a recluse. I'm not sure of his medical diagnosis but he uses a wheelchair that is pushed by a nurse whenever I see him entering or leaving the building. He usually avoids eye contact with the other tenets in the building, obviously not wanting to interact with them. I've always greeted him with a friendly hello but he consistently responds reluctantly with a mere nod of his head, then quickly turns his head away from looking directly at you, which sort of squashes any further attempts to converse with him. I don't think this is a brazen gesture to be rude but merely a manifestation of shyness or possibly depression. Nevertheless, whichever behavior it is, he appears to be uncomfortable around others. Last year, Ginny and I worked during the summer at Maimonides Medical Center on 10th Avenue in Brooklyn, where we both were able to obtain summer internship working in the physical therapy department. We saw all types of disabilities and injuries in the patients who received physical therapy rehabilitation at the clinic. Some had lost limbs during military action in wars; others received their injuries from automobile accidents or sustained them on their jobs. Notwithstanding the cause of their infirmity, a great many, in general, exhibited signs of depression. But not all; there were some with a furious ambition to conquer their disabilities.

JOHN

Two bursts of white lights explored before John, in rapid succession, and he blinked his eyes in fear before he realized that there was no light but just darkness. He was immobilized; laying flat on his back on his hospital bed in his bedroom. The lights had only been a flashback memory of his last day in Afghanistan when he had sustained his life altering injury, which left him a paraplegic. He was suffering multiple flashbacks per week now that he had moved from the rehab facility in Mid-Manhatten to his present apartment in Williamsburg, Brooklyn. The flashbacks were always of the exact moment of the explosion that destroyed the Humvee he and four other soldiers were traveling in, on a dirt road in Afghanistan, that fateful day; and which left him a paraplegic and killed the other men. He never recalled the moment before the explosion or what happened immediately after. It was with some determination that he was able to force his memory to bring back to mind those initial days of hospitalization at the Pakistan International Hospital.

Listening to the night sounds surrounding him now, he could hear the slow, soft snoring of the night male nurse who slept in the bedroom next to his. He now laid awake just staring into the darkness of his room. His thoughts were on his home town in Tennessee, where he had played varsity football at Chattanooga College, before joining the Army. Laying in his hospital bed now, he could almost, in his mind, feel the spasms of aching, overworked muscles resulting from an exhaustive workout or a strenuous played game, during those college years. But in reality he could feel nothing from his lower trunk to his toes. In college, he had played boldly, never worrying about possible traumatic injuries occurring. With no fear, he played the Linebacker position which is a defense position; never suffering any major injury. After school, he had worked briefly as a car salesman at Trendy Auto Sales. Advancement was slow and before long, he started feeling patriotic and decided he would join the army. Many family members had tried to talk him out of joining the military but he was hell bent on fighting in America's war in the Middle East. He had felt pride when he first put on his uniform and looked in the mirror. After basic training his unit was sent to Fort Briggs first, then eventually he was sent to Afghanistan's Bagram Air Base where the army lends support to this largest U.S. military base in AFGHANISTAN. He survived his first tour, but was sent for a second tour in the country. It was during his second tour that he was injured and received his purple heart. By this time his father had died (his mother had died a few years prior to his dad) and his sister had moved to England to work as an Architect. After sustaining his injury the Army had placed him in a Pakistan Hospital for his first hospitalization and rehab, before later shipping him to Mid Manhatten. Now the doctors felt he was able to try living in his own apartment with around the clock nursing care.

His helplessness and dependency on others left him feeling deficient as a man. He had come home from the war feeling disillusioned by what he had seen in Afghanistan; what seemed to be senseless killing and hardships, for civilians as well as many soldiers. "The local people just want to be left alone, they are tired of war", these are the sentiments of most of the soldiers fighting in Afghanistan and Iraq along with John, he felt. John's injury further left him bitter and resentful because of his inability to express his rage towards what the war had cost him.

He hated to look at himself in the mirror to shave because he saw a haunted version of his former self. He had blue eyes that now looked dull instead of vibrant and happy like before. His mouth formed a frown that deepened the sadness of his appearance. He hadn't been in touch with his sister and felt no inclination to do so or for trying to communicate with any of his old friends, who had gradually drifted away, dued mostly to his reluctance to see them and their not knowing how to interact with him. They somehow felt guilty about their own healthy bodies and the limitations of his. They respected the sacrifice that he had made fighting for the prevention of another terrorist attack after 911; but after the killing of Bin Laden, which was one of the goals of the invasion and the capture or killing of Al-Qaeda leaders; like John they wondered what was the purpose of their country still fighting in Afghanistan for these endless years. U.S. troops were now fighting a new enemy. the Taliban, When would all the madness end? To John it would never end. His mind switched to a scene, a memory, before his first tour to Afghanistan; He laid close to his girlfriend, Cassandra, on top of a light weight blanket on the white sand of the Fregate Island Beach in the Seychelles, located east of the African Coast in the Indian Ocean; during a summer vocation they spent together. They listened to music on a battery operated radio entirely happy and content, watching the waves of the ocean tumble vigorously onto the white sand of the beach. There was a subtle breeze that gently lifted Cassandra's hair as it blew across her head. Listening to the music, enjoying the breeze, they talked about a future together. Cassandra said she wanted at least three children and John expressed his desire to wait until he finished his first tour of duty overseas, before they got married and started a family. With their different perspectives they finally agree to do as John wished. When the time came, things took a different path; John decided to do another tour and save his Army salary to be able to buy a house when they got married. Again fate stepped in and John was severely wounded, and spent long months in various facilities where he struggled to overcome his new physical obstacles. His girlfriend Cassandra made many attempts to visit him but the relationship was not able to sustain itself and started disintegrating because of John's aloof response to Cassandra whenever he allowed her to visit him. There was fear for both of them, and they were tormented by their new circumstances. John was determined to drive her away, feeling that he couldn't burden her with such difficult challenges of being a mate for him in his present condition. Cassandra felt she had enough strength and courage to face a future with him, irrespective of how incredibly difficult it might be; she felt a life with him would be new and natural. There were many frequent calls though out the day when she would hesitatingly call him, hopeful but doubtful, that he would accept her calls. She knew he loved her; at least this belief was what drove her to continue to call him, though his repeated failure to accept most of her calls, left a small persistent fear that her belief was unfounded. Meanwhile he would not acknowledge to her or himself that he was being irrationale. He let his self doubt, about his ability to be the mate that she needed, control every decision regarding his interaction or failure to interact with her. The weeks went by, then the months, until it turned into years, at which time neither one of them were sure of what they felt. She would look at the phone, consumed with anger; why didn't he call her, it was always that she had to initiate any contact between the two of them and frankly she didn't have the energy anymore. She was determined that he had to grow up and let her know that she was important to him. Love had to be a two way street - there had to be a reciprocal relationship between them. The futility of the situation overwhelmed her and he suspected that but would not motivate himself to change it.

TAMARA'S JOURNAL ENTRY

It's almost two weeks since I've encountered the young man named Manny and I have to confess, each time I leave my apartment, I secretly hope I see him again. I know it's silly to be so fixated on someone I don't really know, but for whatever reason, I have a quiet yearning in my soul for this encounter to happen. I haven't even told Ginny or my mom (both of whom I tell practically everything) about these unfathomable feelings I have about Manny. How can a person's sensibilities be so affected by one meeting with another person. I don't really even know what I hope will happen if Manny and I meet again. One moment I'm lost in a fantasy about him; us embracing, kissing gently, and the next moment thinking what a fool I am for such silly thoughts. Have I been indoctrinated with some sort of imagined Romeo and Juliet scenario, by all the romantic movies that I have watched late at night on T.V. on the weekends. I guess it is every girl's dream, to find the one true love of her life, get married and live the idyllic life of the perfect marriage.

An elderly retired Jewish couple resides in the same apartment building as my mother and I, and from all outwards appearance, they actually seem to have achieved such marital bliss. I see them holding hands strolling together going through the neighborhood, laughing at each other's remarks, totally involved in each other. Their children are all grown and have left the nest; two sons who have their own families and live in Queens, come often to visit the parents. I've seen little children with them and I suppose these are the grandchildren. So from what I can see, this elderly couple have been blessed. They have found each other, their perfect match, and now are leading a life that many people would envy. They don't seem to have any blemish on their union; it has produced a happy, harmonic, envious relationship by all appearance. They spend a lot of time doing things together. I've seen them all pile up in their car, toting picnic baskets and bicycles plus other items like basketballs, etc. which are thrown into the car trunks and some attached and secured onto the top of the cars. Everyone looks ecstatic as they depart from the neighborhood, off to whatever destination planned for that day. Yes it does seem they have found and are living the idyllic life of the perfect marriage.

THE ROSENSHEINS

Shannah Rosenshein quickly gathered her husband's shirt and necktie from the bedroom's bureau drawer and arranged them neatly on the bedroom bed, along with his smoothly ironed pants, that she had gotten up early to press. Looking at everything neatly laid out on the bed; she was satisfied. Her Joshua would look just fine today. Today was an important date. Hopefully it was to be a milestone in her and her husband's life. They would again have to travel into the cold, sterile, clinical environment of the Oncology Clinic at the Martindale Health Center located ten miles away in Weehawken, New Jersey. It wasn't a long journey by car, but to the Rosensheins its distance seemed longer than it actually was. This was no doubt due to their stress about the reality of Joshua's health and the devastating prognosis that they were told was a possibility.

Two hours later, Shannah and Joshua were at the entrance to the Hospital, bracing themselves for what might be told to them today. Hurriedly they moved through the halls of the lower level and came to the wing of the main building, where the elevators leading up to the Oncology Clinic were located. After a brief wait, The elevator descended and they got in, arriving quickly to the third floor, where they exit the elevator. After checking in at the reception desk, they sat in the comfortable chairs arranged in rows facing the reception desk. Within minutes Joshua's name was called by a nurse and they quickly followed her into the examination room. Dr. Banks arrived a few minutes later and greeted them.

Shannah looked into Joshua's eyes as the doctor gave them the results of the latest brain scan. Relief flooded her, she was jubilant. The news was good; there was still no sign of a return of cancer. The tumor had not regrown. Joshua was grateful too for the welcome news and didn't want to admit, even to himself, just how strainful the waiting for the results had been for him. The past two years of following strict adherence to the protocol for his treatment, had required a resiliency that he would have never thought he was capable of having.

He embraced Shannah as he thanked the doctor for the dedicated care of the medical team which had helped him survive his cancer. The doctor told him he would need to be routinely monitored to ensure that the cancer had not returned. Standing in the doctor's office, Joshua recalled the first doctor visit when he and Shannah had heard the frightening diagnosis; he had a brain tumor. It was not unexpected though; for months Joshua had been experiencing increasingly strong headaches, loss of balance, blurred vision, difficulty walking, problems with coordination and then a mild seizure that confirmed to them that the diagnosis that they had been given by all the other health providers during that initial beginning of symptoms had to be wrong; so they inquired of friends and were directed to neurologist Stan Banks, who finally properly diagnosis the condition.

The doctor recounted what they should expect from the course of the protocol he wished to start Joshua on; with the hope that it would eventually halt the growth of his tumor and maybe shrink it also. He described the treatment course with medical jargon that Joshua and Shannah determinedly tried to follow. His words resonated authoritative confidence that gave them hope; a hope that there would be a successful outcome. They had gone home and pushed back the escalating fears that they shamefully felt they had allowed to torment them, which as devoted Jews, they felt showed a lack of faith. They vowed to trust God; faithfully they went to their community synagogue for public worshiping and gatherings. They kissed their hands and touched the Mezuzah as a sign of respect and blessing as they entered their home. (The Mezuzah is a small box or tube that is attached to the doorpost on the right side of the door of a Jewish home. It traditionally has a casting made of metal, glass, pottery or any other type of waterproof material. Inside it is a scroll upon which is written the passages from Deuteronomy 6:4-9 and 11:13-21 which affirms God's existence and oneness.) They dutifully deposited their contribution funds in the Tzedakah box in the family room. The money was entirely reserved to be given for those in need. This form of giving is called Tzedakakah considered an act of Righteousness or justice. Tzedakah. The amount given is traditionally ten percent. Faithfully they did these things not to bargain with God, but to honor him, for they truly felt that God had blessed them in spite of what the future might bring. They had a profoundly happy life together; the years had been good to them, filled with many wonderful memories; their lavish wedding after months of courtship, the joy at each birth of their two sons, the years rising and guiding their sons from childhood to adulthood and all the many firsts accomplishments their boys experienced was also experienced by them with complete joy. Now there was the fulfillment of seeing their grandchildren start their lives and today's good news boostered their hope for continued time together as a family. Happily they went home and praised God.

One night, three weeks after hearing the good news of Joshua's remission, the couple was relaxing in the kitchen after dinner and discussing the report of multiple suspicious fires occurring throughout the city that was reported on the evening news show on channel WKZM. The anchorman had spoked in dramatic details about various recent fires that were occuring with increased frequency throughout the city. The local newscast show had shown the arson investigator; a balding, lean man in his fifties, who told of the extensive damage the fires had caused and the financial cost they had incurred in the process. Shannah whistled loudly and exclaimed,

"What a shame, for what reason would someone do such a thing? Thank God, Joshua that so far no life has been lost.", Shannah went on "Why, dear God, so senseless".

"This could be the work of some radical activist group bent on inflicting some sort of revenge for harm done to their people, or for views that are contradictory towards their ideology", Joshua explained with patience.

"Well, Joshua, maybe you are right, but again even if it is for revenge, the extent of their anger, to do such mischief I think is going too far", Shannah stressed with conviction of her view point.

Joshua, reached across the table and dipped his knife into the bowl of chatzilim, that Shannah had prepared as an appetizer for dinner, and spread a generous amount on a piece of BAGEL, that Shannah had baked. He slowly munched on the Bagel and smiled at his wife.

"Yes, it would seem so; after all, what is gained by intense hate but the weakening of the health and the well being of the hater. But there is so much injustice and suffering in the world. And it is a fact that Hurt people are known to generally end up hurting other people. This is the deadly trap of Satan. He affects our minds with the thought to strike out in revenge for the pain and hurt that has been inflicted on us", Joshua expressed with spiritual truth.

"Satan has stirred up hate which definitely leads to sin. Men have not yet learnt to love. As Leviticus 19:18 states,

"Do not seek revenge or bear a grudge against one of your people, but Love your neighbor as yourself. I am the Lord". This is God's Command to us his children. We have not been faithful in keeping it. So many of us have neglected the harm done to many of God's children. Many live in extreme poverty that others seem not to care about." Joshua paused and then breathed deeply, as if he felt the pain of poverty himself. " Many live in torn communities that have been ravaged by drugs; crumbled houses leveled by bombs that are no longer fit to live in and certainly not fit to raise a family in. Is a young baby or child supposed to be safe, walking admiss the sharp rubbles.? Certainly not. So again, hurt people,as the saying goes, hurt people". Joshua sighed as he said this, deeply concerned about the world situation and challenges facing man. He remembered the heartbreaking story of a young Asian gymnast, who while practicing on gym equipment-he wasn't sure if it was the balancing beam, but the young girl lost her balance and fell off the equipment, injuring herself severely. She was paralyzed from the neck down. He couldn't imagine such hardship for one so young to bear.

"Shannah, remember the story of the young gymnast, who became paralyzed? She was Asian I believe". Shannah nodded yes.

"Well, imagine her emotional pain and suffering. Her parents must have had to feel resentment for their child's tragic fate. These things of life can cause bitterness and hate. You can end up just hating everything. God had to know she was very strong; her life is an encouragement to us all; no matter what we are going through, can it compare to her ordeal?". Joshua then looked at Shannah closely, searching her eyes.

"Whatever happens we must never forget the book of Joshua from the Old Testament of the Holy Bible, chapter one, verse nine (Joshua 1:9), which states 'For the Lord your God is with you wherever you go'".

Shannah inhaled and trembled slightly. "Yes. Joshua, you are right. Life is stuff and indeed more so for many. I will try to not pass judgement on these people responsible for the fires".

"That's fine Shannah. That's fine. Never forget".

THE FIRES

The demons will want to keep their eyes on the elderly. For they fear their wisdom and faith.

Along the waterfront, huge misshapen prickly ears of a giant demonic dragon heard the conversation of the elderly Rosensheins and it laughed with unbound glee. Fellow demons, of assorted sizes, crowded around it and they all bellowed and grunted their pleasure at the immense success of the arsonists, they had manipulated, in bringing more chaos, confusion and misery into men' existence. They swelled in anticipation at the actions of two newest recruits they were misleading and controlling. The two young men were setting up basic necessary apparatus for tonight's planned FIRE. Swiftly they worked, securing the inflammable devices in the most effective locations within the empty warehouses. The locations of the incendiaries had to be well planned to optimize the quickest burn, most intense heat and surest annihilation of the cause of the fire. Demons whispered encouraging directions and instructions into the young men's minds, leading them like sheeps or pieces of a broad game; happy to bring evil to fruition. They clicked their teeth together, inpatient for the eventual burning infernos that would be blazing dangerously along the waterfront destroying the warehouse properties of greedy owners. They laughed in contempt at men's greed; how God must be disappointed in his creation, they snickered. All the merchandise cramped into these vast buildings will scorch and sizzle in the spreading howling flames. The many buildings could possibly crumble and collapse. This vision excited the demons further. These happenings would surely discourage men and bring unbridle anger and a quest for retaliatory revenge. For after all, the owners placed untold value in their possessions and wealth they represent. The demons were fully aware how men would react to their shenanigans. With the success of tonight's mischief they would proceed to the next step on their agenda, but they recognize the need to keep a vigilant watch on the saints, especially the elderly ones like the Rosensheins or the man, Raul. They were capable of untold resourcefulness facilitated by their zealous prayers.

The demons could not confuse them in general with their usual cleverness. The problem was that they consolidated their spiritual power by communal fellowship and prayers. Another problem loomed large on the horizon; the potential of the young teen, Tamara. She was now venturing into journal writing. The possibility exists that she could write a novel. The demons concurred, they must definitely keep a surveillance on her.

JOHN

John was seated in front of his living room window which looked out onto Wassail Street, the broad avenue running west to east along the central part of Williamsburg. The physical therapist had completed the morning workout with him in his second bedroom which served as his physical therapy space and had a pull out bed where his night nurse slept. His regular day nurse had locked the front door after the physical therapist had left and was busy tidying up the apartment before it was time to help John eat his lunch. He had left John in the living room, in front of the large window that faced out onto the avenue in front of the apartment building. John was accustomed to staring out of his window at the people walking on the sidewalk and his fellow neighbors entering and leaving the building. He would glance from behind his curtain with his face hidden by the branches of the old oak tree which stood to the side of his window. This activity, besides watching T.V. for most of the day, was his primary distraction from the boredom he felt almost constantly week after week. His nurse had subscribed to the daily newspaper for him, but John usually refused to even look at them and the nurse ended up reading them and throwing them out with the trash on garbage pickup day. John didn't want to know what was going on in the world and certainly didn't want to read anything about war.

He also did not look at the news shows on T.V. preferring to stay numb and only watched game shows where there wasn't a constant enactment of real life conditions that he was no longer a partaker of. He didn't want to watch depictions of idealized family life or even to see dysfunctional ones either; neither did he want to see the medical drama shows where there were vivid reminders of the fragility of human life, of all life forms. He sort not to witness men's cruelty to each other demonstrated by the various crimes they committed on the numerous law enforcement shows that were portrayed on most networks.

Yes, he acknowledged, most popular T.V. shows were difficult for him to watch. But unoccupied by television, there were the overwhelming feelings of depression that engulfed him at random unexpected times; while watching a mother bird feed her young babies in the nest of the branches of the oak tree outside his apartment building; hearing the laughter of young children running and screaming as they played outside,

Last night he felt it too as he watched the young black mother, whose children called her Nettie, walking to the building, dressed smartly as always, in the company of a young Black man John never saw before. He watched as Nettie smiled brightly as she glanced periodically at her companion as they strolled slowly laughing and talking, preoccupied in their mutual enjoyment of their conversation, walking in close proximity to each other. John had felt the sting of depression gripped him as he watched; the loneliness of the past three years came at him like a tidal wave.

Like a tidal wave it knocked all the breath out of him at once, filled his lungs, replacing the air that should have been there, suffocating him. Like a tidal wave, within seconds it immersed his whole body in its power and he felt disconnected to his surroundings. He had grieved for his inability to walk along side the woman he loved, to hold Cassandra in his arms, to hear her laughter that he had thought would always be his right to enjoy; their little intimaticies that he never would have imagined could not exist to eternity. The grieve was so profound, it was the only thing in his reality. There was no other being for him. It persisted, it seemed a lifetime. It was heavy, a million tons of weight upon him. He had stared off into nothingness.

Now, sitting alone at the window he remembered how Cassandra had tried so hard to connect with him those first initial months during his hospital stay; he now wondered if his stubbornness in blocking her approaches, personified a weakness in his character. He sighed, resigned to the realization that he was incapable of changing any yesterdays; the past stood irrevocable to change.

This morning he had watched his blind neighbor Raul as he had left the building; he was walking slowly with his walking cane and listening to music coming from a small, portable radio secured on his waist in a fanny pack. John recognized the words of the song being played on the radio as the lyrics to "O Holy Night". The music was stirring and the singer's voice radiated with equal stirring divinity. John had watched his neighbor's face as he walked along, humming the music as he went. It struck John that Raul's face expressed a serene ecstasy inspired by the soaring message of the song. John felt a mystifying desire to connect to the source of his neighbor's obvious happiness. The concept of happiness in his present condition seemed fleeting, if anything. He wondered how his life might have been if he had not gone to Afghanistan; if he had stayed in Chattanooga, Tennese, married Cassandra and raised a family. He had been so certain about his convictions of the rightness of his viewpoint about the need to destroy the enemy (his concept of the Taliban Milita, that took control of Afghanistan from early 1996). He felt it patriotic to defend his country, America and all that he believed it stood for. Now he was uncertain. The utter loneliness of his existence brood on him day and night; this is what the war had caused him. At that moment his eye rested on a book of Poetry by Teddy Ramsey that he had read last night. It was opened to the poem, "In the silence of Winter".

IN THE SILENCE OF WINTER

It is always a time of mourning
when love has departed
A part of you
leaves mysteriously with it

Some say your life is never the same
& the circumference of the world
seems smaller
insignificant

If love leaves in winter
when days are cold
with snow gently falling
loneliness seem everywhere

The minutes of the long day
evolve to hours
hours to days
days to weeks
time becomes lost frozen
It is an agony unbearable

Nia Ramsey

when love has departed
In the gloom of winter
your heart becomes a flame

for

the

tears

silently

falling

THE FIRES

The city fire stations were on high alert, they braced themselves for the next excruciating arsonists' fire. These mysterious arsons were devastating in the monetary loss they accounted for and the extensive areas they covered. The firefighters were overwhelmed and exhausted, spending additional man hours to accomplish what looked like a futile attempt to stay ahead of the arsonists; in preventing harm to the citizens of the city.

Immersed in the backdrop of each fire, were the ever present demons; no one saw them but they slashed with their sharp claws penetrating the sturdiest structures and hearts of the arsonists, shredding any emotion of sympathy for the potential harm to the safety of the inhabitants of the buildings they burned. Tonight, again they stealthily roamed the rooftops of the city's buildings squawking and hissing as their eyes glistened like white alabaster, intensely focused on finding the next suitable site for a ferocious fire. They wanted an all out effort by all their demonic hosts. So far word was emanating among legions of them and bouncing along throughout the ranks, and they gathered in large groups, hissing their rage; evil, their intent; shifty-eyed they swiftly set about conjuring up their most potent magical arsenals and spells.

To capture the minds of their potential arsonists, the diversity of spells - some unique, others quite familiar and ordinary - had to be created.

Tonight's fire on the Brooklyn Waterfront fulfilled all they had envisioned in their planning. Astonishingly the two young recruits did a masterful job; the fire they started left the waterfront desolate along the path of the fire. Approximately, 15 minutes after the first sighting of flames, along the northern end of the waterfront, a roaring, rapidly spreading bright orange, red wall of flames - a four alarmer - alerted five fire houses and multiple fire trucks, rescue trucks, pumpers and ambulances were dispatched to the area. By the time they had arrived, the fire had spread across blocks of warehouses, garages and other buildings, threatening to spread farther. The two young arsonist recruits were quite a distance away from the fire, but close enough to hear the responding fire and rescue vehicles as they roared down the streets and arrived at the location of the fire. The young men were filled with elation at what they speculated they had managed to accomplish this evening. All the rage they had inside them from years of escalating hardship and loss to them and the other arsonists, found some release, like the top being taken off a boiling pot. The pot still boiled, but the built up pressure inside was now able to escape. The two young men turned away from watching the wall of flames and black, bellicose smoke and hurried to the prearranged location where they meet other young men and some young women along with a few older individuals who were united in their quest of reckoning with the perceived enemy. They were agitated and quite unaware of the host of evil presences surrounding them and gliding directly over them; just as or even more agitated than they were.

The two new recruits, Emil and Samuel, joined the mass of arsonists gathered together to brief each other on what had been going on in the city these past months.

Emil asked Samuel if they were careful enough tonight.

"Do you think anyone might have seen us?" He asked urgently, with a little apprehension in his voice.

"Emil, you and I were very careful. Don't worry we did an excellent job. But listen, the supreme leader is speaking now", Samuel said and directed his attention to the front of the hall where the meeting was taking place. All eyes in the brightly lit room looked towards the speaker, up front. His voice boomed with self righteous authority.

"Our efforts have proven ideal. Much has been accomplished these past few weeks. Surely we are being given the right direction to take" the speaker, the group's leader said as he paused and directed his gaze from left to right, appearing to see everyone's face in the audience and directing his comments to each person directly. He stood erect, at 6 feet and 4 inches, powerfully built with wide shoulders and massive arms that though motionless at the moment, did not conceal their deadly potential; if unbridled to engage in battle. His frame was that of a warrior with strong, bulging thighs. But this physical superiority did not in itself establish his right to lead, it was secondary to his intellectual capability that far out strided the level of other persons of high intellect. His name was Leon and his followers called him "The Lion".

The audience was quiet, fully captivated by his every utterance. With the skill of a master battle strategist, he explained the necessary scrimmages that would be employed in his vision for success in their undertaking, to be victorious in finalizing this master plan agenda.

KWUAME

One week since his excursion downtown with his friend Nat, Kwuame now laid stretched out on his couch, listening to the music he had purchased, his mind speculating about the pivotal role of Blacks Artists in Music History. Much of different cultures' music has been greatly influenced by Blacks and their music; from the music introduced by Aricans during slavery, to the music created by Afro Americans in America, Kwuame reflected. Again, he thought how lucky it was to have been able to find the works of Black musicians he admired.

With his mind on the music and his eyes on the Help Wanted Ads in the Daily Chronicler, he tried to concentrate on the ads, trying to give them his priority. He found that the endless roles of ads were becoming blurry as he swiftly scanned them, one by one, dismissing most as jobs needing qualifications that he didn't have. He saw ads for accountants, Art Director, Account Support Specialist, Customer Service Associate, Electronic Technician, Environmental Service Director, Health Care Scheduler, Investigator, Medical Records Director, Office Manager, Phlebotomist, Truck Driver Jobs - Local CDL, ETC., etc.... He spotted one ad that looked promising. In bold, standout print, it stated "CLIMB THE LADDER OF SUCCESS". Blinking his tired eyes, he read, "We're looking for motivated people, who are energetic and wish to join our team of Customer Service Representatives. You will take inbound calls at our new Long Island Call Center Facility". The ad further stated "HOURS ARE FLEXIBLE. WE ARE OPEN FROM 8:00 AM to 10:00 PM and we provide the training you will need". The job offered not only paid training but also paid vacation and benefits like medical/dental/vision coverage. Kwuame's interest abruptly came to a halt as he read further, the ad stated that you had to have previous customer service and sales experience, and be able to type 60 WPM.

"Great", Kwuame thought defeatedly. The ad plainly offers to give you training, then in the next instant is insisting that you have to have previous experience. What the hell kind of jive is that? Kwuame threw the newspaper on the floor and marched into his kitchen to get a bottle of coke from the refrigerator. taking a long sip of the cool, refreshing soda, he considered if he should continue his job search when basically he felt an intense inclination to just quit. He knew he was capable of handling school and a job, with the intention of saving up money for college expenses at New York University, located in Manhatten. He hoped to be able to apply soon, if only he was able to surmount these freaking obstacles that were making his goals incredibly difficult to obtain. Wholly wrapped up in his dilemma of what he should do next, he didn't hear the knocking at his door until it grew louder as the person knocking increased the pounding he was exerting.

Finally aware of the noise at his door, Kwuame immediately

rushed to the door to see who was there. Looking through the peep hole, he saw his uncle Khaalig. Opening the door, he greeted him warmly.

"Man, I'm glad to see you, Uncle, I was thinking about calling you", Kwuame exclaimed, as he hugged his uncle.

Uncle Khaaliq was a tall, somewhat skinny man, with a gangly physique, On his chin he sported a goatee that was bushy and salt and pepper like his Afro hair cut. He was 6'5" and he came from a family known for its exceptionally tall males (the women of the family were not as tall, except for his sister Carol) He was Kwuame's mother's oldest brother. Kwuame resembled him around the eyes, which were penetrating and reflected intellectual keenness (he perceived the slightest interchange between people around him, seeming to know their intentions). His forehead was large and his skin a deep, rich brown mahogany. There was a slight hint of a dimple on his left cheek which was not duplicate on his right cheek. Kwuame had found him intriguing as he watched him over the years. He had an urgency about him in everything he did. This was probably why he joined the Black Panther Party during his youth, Kwuame reflected. His uncle did not want to wait on the system of things in America to change slowly to bring about equality for his people; he felt that white racism would not allow that to happen, that Blacks had to demand fair and equal employment, descent safe housing and the Black Panther Party wanted to see an end to the draft. The Party's free breakfast Program was enthusiastically approved by him; young minds had to be nourished in order to be effective. He had given Kwuame his copy of Black Panther Leader Eldridge Cleaver's Book of essays,

"Soul on Ice" as a present on his 13th Birthday. The Book was Cleaver's despliction of Society's imprisonment of men's souls. His uncle had given him other books that were the embodiments of his personal dogma or belief system and Kwuame reverently read them all, gratefully trying to grasp what they offered. He particularly admired the poems "Catharsis" as well as "Lovescape", by Teddy Ramsey. He had read the Book "Bury my Heart at Wounded Knee" by Dee Brown and felt the pain of the Native American Indian survivors of the White man's conquest of the American West, as if it was his own. From another offering of his uncle, Kwuame had read the remarks of Joe Louis, the Heavy Weight Boxer (1914-1981) that was published in an article, that said "Rev. J.H.Maston..talked and through my fighting I was to uplift the spirit of my race. I must make the whole world know that Negro people were strong, fair and decent", and was impressed with what Mr Louis had gone though.

Kwuame now watched as his uncle Khaalig's eyes looked around his apartment and rested on the newspaper.

"Why is the newspaper scattered all over the floor, is this some sort of new look?" Khaaliq asked.

Kwuame bent over and reached to pick up the Newspaper he had thrown down earlier in frustration.

"Just was expressing my anger at not being able to find a promising lead for a job in any of the want ads in it", Kwuame lamented.

He bundled up the newspaper and placed it on the coffee table, then sat down on the couch, frowning. Limply he dropped his hands on his thighs. Khaaliq looked at him, sympathetically and sat down on a chair facing the couch.

"Yeah, that is a problem for a lot of people", Khaalig acknowledged. I've been discussing challenges of finding work with some brothers recently, as a matter of fact". Khaaliq went on.

"Many are at the breaking point and need immediate serious relief. There's the situation of not having the necessary education or training for quite a few job seekers".

Kwuame nodded his head in agreement.

"Yes, I saw an ad for a job that I figured I could possibly handled. It promised paid training on the job, then in the next few sentences it listed experiences that you had to have to be able to get the job. Talk about squashing a person's hope", Kwuame grimaced in utter resentment.

"I hear you, Kwuame but I don't think the solution is to be dormant and not try to reverse the disparity between opportunities offered to the public", Khaaliq said with seriousness.

"There's information available that you have to search for. Obscured offers are available, if you know where to look. Not everyone has access to them. I've been doing some due diligence, researching on the internet and I am seeking to get funding to start a service to offer financial aid and scholarship information to the public. I'm retired now and I know some brothers who might be interested in assisting me with this venture". Khaaliq had his usual inclination towards urgency as he mapped out his sequence of aspirations he envisioned.

"Not everyone has a computer and might have some difficulty in getting to a place, like a library, which has computers for the public to use. Lacking this access, a person can be handicapped in even finding job offers online. I'm glad to see that you are still buying a newspaper and utilizing their help wants ads. Now the next step is getting the necessary training to be able to compete for the jobs. Education has to be stressed to our families", he continued.

"Employment for everyone is not just a Black person's struggle. It's every one's struggle. Whites, not withstanding, the advantage of their race, also need to collaborate on this effort. A lot of them are also facing economic difficulties too. Your mom told me of a white co-worker who is in her 70's who is still working as an office aid because she never made enough salary during her years of working to get a decent amount of social security to live off when it was time for her to retire". You see a lot of older workers, hustling at jobs they can hardly handle", Khaaliq said, looking intensely into his nephew's eyes.

Kwuame shrugged, surprised to hear his uncle's comments. He felt Blacks still had it harder than most other races. He sat quietly listening to his uncle, not wanting to contradict him, but profoundly concerned more about the plight of his own race to think with discernment about some other race.

"Pardon me, Uncle, but I think you have to admit the Black man has historically suffered economically more than any other race. We were brought over to this country to do back breaking work for free. We suffered through hot weather forced to bring in the crop for white farmers. Our women had to leave their children in the care of someone else while they labored in the fields. Nat and I read about the early childhood of Frederick Douglass. His mother was sent to a plantation every day that was 12 miles away, where she had to work. Only a few times was she able to walk home in time to see Frederick to bed. She died when Frederick was seven years old."

"Yes that is true", Khaaliq admitted, and continued, "He was left parentless (his father was unknown) and if it wasn't for his slave master's daughter, Lucretia Auld, who took some interest in him and sent him to Baltimore to be her nephew's companion, where he learned to read and write, he might not have been able years later to write "The Narrative of the Life of Frederick Douglass", Khaaliq said, and then went further in his effort to teach his nephew.

"What you're saying is factual, that's essentially why I had joined the Black Panther Party in my youth. They were trying to correct the injustice inflicted on Blacks. Yes, our treatment has been unparalleled except for the treatment of Jews", Khaaliq stopped speaking suddenly with a look of instant reflection. "Wait, I need to rethink that. There is also the awful plight of the Native Americans, the American Indians. Their story has been one of massive injustice also", Khaaliq corrected himself.

"As you remember from the book I gave you, written by Dee Brown, concerning the history of injustice suffered by them", Khaaliq added, and then went on,

"I've tried to enlighten you over the years about things that are not taught to you and every other student in the classroom. That goes not only for the classrooms of America, but also thoughout the school systems of practically all nations, if not all. Many of our black brothers have traveled to other countries; men like Malcom

X, and writers such as Richard Wright and James Baldwin, and many others; they have seen and experienced what concepts, some misleading, the world has of the Black race. But there are also a lot of misrepresenting of many things that people really have taken to be truths about each other". Khaalig leaned back in his chair causing it to squeak with the sudden shift of his weight, pushing against the shiny hardwood floor it rested on. Khaalig, now settled more comfortably, continued his narrative.

"What has the Irish been portrayed as? Many people believe they are habitual hard drinkers (drunkards) or at least at one time they were believed to be so", Khaaliq explained, then went on.

"Going back to the Native American Indian, as an example. they were repeatedly described in films and books as savages, bent on killing the white man, when in actuality they not only tried and believed that they could live in peace with the white race; they signed documents after documents (treaties) with the intent in bringing about peace. They believed what they signed, what they thought were compromises giving them land where they could live; and were time after time disappointed with the realization that the whites would not honor the treaties they signed", Khaalig let this information sink in, then continued,

"Sometime, I used to cry in pain at the lost years that I could have been honoring God with my talents. Did you know that I wanted to be a construction worker, learn to build houses? This dream was never realized. There weren't many opportunities or job jobs offered to Black men in the building trade during my youth and even at this present time the jobs are limited. I have a friend who was one of the lucky ones, he was able to be a bricklayer and helped in the building of many buildings. But I realize that there have been, could be, will be many young, old people who also never reach the intended purpose or plan for their lives (God's plan), because of War, poverty, hatred, illness, and I think of the years of millions of God's children in Africa, South America, all over the world in the area the world calls the "Third World"; but also here in America (the place considered The Greatest Country) some people because of the obstacles that they face, also never reach their full potentials. Then I think how dare I feel self pity for myself. Who crys for all these millions, perhaps billions of God's children. The children who have freedom from the plights that I mentioned, need to bend down and pick up these lives. The popular saying "bend down and pick yourself up by your bootstraps" is wrong!!! When these people because of their lack don't even have bootstraps. So for whatever time I have left here in God's created world, I will try to raise awareness about what too many of the world's people have ignored. I hope I can appeal to mankind to give all people a chance for resurrected New Lives where they also can glorify God with displaying all the Beauty he has given them. Where through their new strengthened lives they achieve oneness of purpose with all God's children: Unity. I also want to be a writer", Khaalig smiled. Kwuame looked at his uncle and reflected on his words.

TAMARA

Tamara squeezed her eyes shut for a few minutes, then opened them and placed her math book down on her desk. Tired after hours of doing homework and studying for a math test, she stood up and stretched, first bending down and touching her toes, then straightening up and raising her arms in the air, trying to loosen up stiff muscles; cramped from sitting down so long. She had been studying organic science, American History and Calculus. She was taking an advanced college preparatory course and the work was hard, but she didn't mind. She loved Science and Math and easily excelled in any math course she took. She also found that history courses fascinated her too. Lately she had been disillusioned with all the evident omission of the inclusions of Black achievements and heroes in the History Books as her friend Kwuame had enlightened her about recently. The contributions to the world by so many talented Black individuals has been totally ignored by historians in America and abroad. She remembered the conversation that she, Ginny, Nat and Kwuame had last month.

"You know there are countless Blacks who haven't gotten their due in history", Kwuame told them while they all were sitting on the stairs of her Brownstone apartment building. Tamara had looked up at Kwuame who was seated a few steps above her.

"What are you talking about?" she said.

"My uncle has been telling me a lot about the numerous inventions and accomplishments of our people that just haven't been told or taught in the school system. Hell, every February the public is told about the same few Blacks that represent Black History. I'm not knocking these Blacks that are mentioned over and over, again, but there are so many more who have done such outstanding achievements and have contributed to a wide range of fields; there are great educators, athletes, writers, poets, politicians, explorers, military heroes, entertainers, singers, labor organizers, Nobel Peace Prize winners, doctors and the list is even more extensive than that. From the same list of individuals they mention every February you would think that we as a people have only a limited presence in history. That's all Bull", Kwuame seemed ready to spew out racial epithets in anger.

"Man, that's wicked, pure racism. It's meant to keep us down. Deny our history and make us feel worthless", Nat joined in, expressing his opinion.

Ginny and Tamara looked from Kwuame to Nat, fascinated by what the guys were saying.

"Why don't they tell of Daniel Hale Williams, who was born in 1856 and died 1931, who was the first doctor to perform a successful open heart operation? Hell, we have great role models just like everyone else. People we can be proud of, to imitate in greatness," Kwuame said bitterly. "And there was Ronald McNair, who was a laser physicist, an accomplished scientist, an African

American who flew on the fatal flight of the Challenger space rocket where he and seven other astronauts were killed within minutes after take off when the space ship exploded; all were killed instantly. While on previous flights, McNair played his saxophone (he was an accomplished musician too)".

The afternoon wore on, with the teens expounding on the many deficiencies of the school system and the inaccuracies of the Historians, past and present, that were doing such an inept job. Kwuame felt there needed to be a whole revamp of every history book utilized by the school system. He said,

"You know there is such a thing as revised Editions for books".

Ginny laughed gaily, "That would be something. Maybe I would be one of those writers they would hire to assemble the research for the Historians and help them to put it in a presentable format". Ginny was an instinctively gifted student of the fundamentals of English grammar and usage. She also attended Tamara's school and was in the advance College Preparatory Program. Her hope was to become an editor in the future.

"Girl, you had better do an excellent job if you do. You know Kwuame and I will be down on you too if you mess up the assignment", Nat joked, poking Ginny's arm in the process of his teasing her.

They all continued conversing and then indulged in the speculation of how much money would have to be appropriated to achieve the undertaking of such a huge commission.

"I think it should be the government's job with help from philanthropists investors", Tamara declared firmly, leaning forward with a determined grim expression on her face.

"There would certainly be some querulous resentments from quite a few people", Ginny interjected. The teens agreed this would be the case, especially among certain groups like White Supremacists; such as the Neo-Nazi, Ku Klux Klan (KKK) and other equally offensive racial hate groups.

They watched the little kids, who were playing hop-scotch in the street in front of them and imagined how different things could be for their lifetime if such fairness and equality could exist for them in the future. The impact would be tremendous. For them to see the value and uniqueness of every person and what they could unleash of their own potential to influence and shape future generations. Everyone striving for success and the goal to be the best that they could be.

The teens had continued talking and sharing ideas and opinions until late in the afternoon. Tamara now recalled that weekend afternoon now in her bedroom as she sat at her desk, taking a needed break from her studies.

"Tamara", Ann called out as she stood outside of Tamara's locked bedroom door, and when Tamara responded with "Yes, Mom", Ann opened the door and told her that there was a young man at the front door asking to speak to her. Nervous and gripped with sincere confusion as to who could be calling on her, Tamara stole a swift glance at her reflection in her bedroom door mirror, checking to see if she looked disheveled. She patted her hair and straightened her blouse which was slipping slightly off one shoulder. Satisfied with her appearance, she hurried past her mom and went into the living room. Standing near the front door was Manny. He cracked a wide smile when he saw her and Tamara smiled too in response, slightly self-conscious, she stuttered a "hello".

"Hope you don't mind but I asked my friend Raul where you lived. I wanted to see you, so here I am. Sorry I've come without being invited. It's okay I hope?" He smiled sheepishly, looking both goofy and irresistibly handsome at the same time. He was imposing in a Black Fleece Hoodie over a royal Blue Crewneck T-Shirt and black cargo pants.

"No, it is alright", Tamara responded, looking bewildered, Then remembering her manners, quickly introduced her mother who had stepped into the room at that moment.

"Mom this is Manny, a friend of our neighbor, Raul. Manny meet my mom, Ann".

Hello Ms Ann", Manny smiled, "nice to meet you"

"Same here Manny, it is a pleasure to meet a friend of Raul", Ann assured Manny.

"If Tamara is finished with her school work, I was just about to announce that dinner is ready, why don't you join us, if that's okay with Tamara", Ann said. Tamara responded feebly,

"I only have a slight bit more work to do and it would be fine with me if Manny joined us", her voice strained, despite her secret joy. Ann told the two to sit down and that she would go and prepare the dining room table for their meal.

Tamara motioned with a wave of her hand for Manny to sit down on the sofa. She sat in a side chair placed next to the sofa. Manny sat and looked around the room. The sofa he sat on was a beautiful Teal Blue color and the window behind the sofa was covered with a sheer white curtain beneath a white and teal Blue patterned drape. There was a matching love seat placed on the right side of the sofa. He noticed various Knicknacks lined up on the shelves of a black bookcase. The bookcase also contained hardcover and paperback books dispersed on some shelves, also Pictures of Tamara and her mother plus pictures of a man Manny assumed must be Tamara's father. He looked a few seconds at the pictures of Tamara's dad, and noticed the similarity between him and Tamara. Manny looked over at one corner of the room and saw a glass desk which held a computer and a fancy white, silver and teal blue lamp, with a white lamp shade. There were abstract pictures done in pastel colors on the walls and the floor was probably original oak hardwood, various other art work and portraits of Black men and women and children were also hung on the walls.

He finally realized that Tamara was watching him closely and he smiled and said,

"You have a nice apartment".

"Thank you" Tamara said. "Where do you live?"

"I live over on Baltic Run near the old railroad crossing on Pacific Street. My brother brought the house for my family after his first year playing professional baseball".

"Wow, for real. Your brother plays professional baseball? What's his name?"

Manny felt a sting of resentment at Tamara's obvious admiration for his brother who she didn't even know.

"His name is Fernando, he plays for the Dodger's"

"Gee, that's great. What about you? Do you play baseball too?"

"I play but not professionally", Manny somehow managed to say without any bitterment. "I'm working at Jay's Delicatessen located downtown, right now, but I'm thinking about going to college at night. I haven't decided what to take yet so I'm putting that on hold". He then asked Tamara what were her interests.

"I enjoy my math and science classes and might pursue a career in those fields but I also like writing and dancing. I attend a dance school located in the Boreum Hill section of Brooklyn".

Tamara smelled her mother's classic meatloaf's appetizing aroma floating into the room from the kitchen. She hoped Manny liked meatloaf, her mother's recipe was a favorite of her's. It was handed down to Ann by her grandmother. It consisted of ground beef mixed with tomato sauce, bread crumbs, egg, onion, then Worcestershire Sauce with thyme, garlic, salt and pepper was added and mixed thoroughly. Then the ingredients were formed into a loaf, brown sugar was then blended with mustard and additional tomato sauce and spread on top of the meatloaf. Sometimes Ann would add chopped green pepper and 1/4 teaspoon ground red and white pepper to the ground beef mixture, changing the flavor slightly. Usually Ann would serve roasted vegetables with baked potatoes as a side to go along with the meatloaf.

Tamara was delighted to have Manny's company as they sat and listened to each other and her happiness seem to overflow with her anticipation for the evening to be even more special with the eating of the meal Ann had prepared. She felt a warmth of peace and rightness, as if God was sanctioning this evening.

Ann called out to them to come into the dining room to eat. When they sat down, Ann lead them in blessing the meal and encouraged the teens to dig in and enjoy the meal. She sliced off a sizable piece of meatloaf and placed it on a plate and passed it to Manny and directed him to help himself to the roasted vegetables that were in a large china bowl placed directly in front of him. Manny thanked her and scooped up the vegetables with the large serving spoon that was inserted in the bowl. There was fresh bread, still hot from the oven, next to the vegetables, already sliced and Manny picked up a slice and then spread some butter on it. Everyone filled their plates and Ann looked on, triumphant in the success of her meal as evident by the concentration of Tamara and Manny as they wolfed the food down. She especially was pleased to watch Manny eat; the young man certainly had a healthy appetite..That would account for his size and muscles she reflected with genuine amusement. Her daughter Tamara was doing a good job of mimicking Manny's appetite, as she shoved spoonful after spoonful of the meal into her mouth.

"Well guys, I guess you enjoy the meal", Ann teased looking at them smiling broadly. The two teens grinned back at her sheepishly and affirmed their pleasure.

"Ms. Ann, this meal is delicious. Pardon me, but when can I be invited again to dinner", Manny mumbled, his mouth overflowing with food, with no qualms about expressing his satisfaction with the meal and desire to visit again.

Tamara laughed along with Ann at Manny's brashness. She watched her mother looking at Manny and wondered what she thought of him. Tamara had only recently been allowed to date, her mother set the age for dating at sixteen, the same age she herself had to reached before grandma allowed her to date. Tamara was a little apprehensive about Ann questioning Manny about himself too inquisitively. She was afraid her mother might put a halt to any further involvement between her and Manny. While they were conversing in the living room, Manny had told her about receiving counseling at the Williamsburg Community Health and Restoration Center (now, recently renamed, The Genesis Awakement Center), where her neighbor Raul worked. He said that was where he had meet Raul. He admitted that he had been in treatment for alcohol and marijuana addiction and now was fully recovered and only receiving life skills training periodically and group therapy with Raul's class to help keep him on course. Tamara's feelings for Manny were untainted by what he told her but she feared the repercussions if her mother was informed of his history. She concluded it would be best not to have it revealed just yet. Gingerly she tried to keep talking and steering the conversation on neutral grounds, averted from too probing topics; she asked Manny about his two younger sisters and questioned him further about his older brother. She vaguely sensed that there was some dormant underlying friction between the two brothers. She supposed it must be daunting to have a sibling who had achieved so much accomplishments. Surely, she hoped, Manny didn't feel insignificant in his brother's shadow. Miraculously Ann apparently was intrigued about Puerto Rico and bombarded Manny with endless questions, asking him about his early years spent in Puerto Rico and what the Island's attractions were. Manny was very cordial and sincerely pleased that she was interested in his homeland. He told her of the endless fun he had kayaking with his cousins in the Island's bays and the days spent on the gorgeous beaches enjoying the warmth of the sun. He loved hiking the mountain trails and enjoyed playing under the waterfall with other Island children in the scorching summer days. Tamara and Ann listened to the excitement in Manny's voice as he reminisced about those years with zeal.

Tamara listened thoughtfully as Manny spoke and wondered why, with such obvious fond memories of early childhood years, Manny's life had taken such a deviant path to alcohol and drug addiction. Was it peer pressure and/or harsh self judgement that caused things to unravel in his life. Could she be doing the wrong thing in not telling her mother what she knew? An avalanche of doubt was entangling her thoughts and she remembered a verse from the Bible, "Surely you desire truth in the inner parts; you teach me wisdom in the inmost place", Psalm 51:6". She had a huge decision to make; she had always trusted her mother and reverently had always gone to God with her problems. But now her mind was blank. What Tamara didn't know was that there was a presence lurking in the dining room, other than her mother and Manny. A little demon had been assigned to watch her and now he waited to see the outcome of Tamara's battle with trust. Would she put her trust in God?

Tamara's mind drifted back to what her mother was now saying

"It was just awful and took all night and into the morning to put out. It obliterated ten blocks of the waterfront", Ann was explaining to Manny.

"Yes, I heard about how it caused so much damage from my

family. And like the other fires, the police have not yet arrested the perpetrators", Manny replied.

"No one was hurt, thank goodness. I pray that who ever is doing this will surrender and stop terrorizing the city". Ann straightened her back, and leaned forward as with determined admonition for the arsonists.

"It is dreadful and they need to abandon this senseless destruction and show some prudence. They will eventually get caught and have to face incarceration in jail or the possibility of getting hurt themselves in one of their fires".

"There's got to be a motive for what they are doing. Usually a crime like this is motivated by the possibility of profit, or for the sake of revenge. And other motives can be to try to cover up other crimes like murder, burglary, and embezzlement", Manny interjected.

"Don't forget the fourth category", Tamara spoke up.

"Some arsonists, known as pyromaniacs, don't have any real rational motive for what they do except for the thrill it gives them, adrenaline rush or a sexual high".

"That is correct", Ann added. "In my psychology class in college, we learned a lot about them. You can not really place them in a specific category. They each can have various pathologies that leads to their condition. Each possible pathology in itself doesn't necessarily cause a person to start a fire, just in the few who do".

A brief fluttering of wings of the listening demon seem to accent the words spoken by Ann. Then the demon leaned forward threatenly, in the far right corner of the dining room, unseen by the humans and huffed vaporeous breathes and continued to listen.

He kept an eye on Tamara. She sit looking uncomfortable and wore a preoccupied expression on her face, not really fully engaged with everything that was said at the table. She still struggled with her heart concerning Manny's past. To get up enough strength and to reveal what she knew would take an abundance of faith. Faith in God to direct the outcome. So with a calm resolve but slightly wobbly trust she chose her words carefully. Interrupting her mother, who was about to say something.

"Mom, Manny knows our neighbor Raul, as I said. He know him from meeting him at the Genesis Awakement Center where Raul works", she said pleasantly smiling at her mom.

Ann looked quizzically at Tamara then Manny. "Oh, Oh... doesn't Raul work at a rehab center?" Ann fumbled slowly.

"Do you work there too, Manny?"

"No Ms. Ramsey.", Raul is my counselor in group therapy. I have successfully completed my individual private therapy and I now receive training within a group setting, where the participants try, under the guidance of a trained counselor, to encourage each other towards establishing healthy goals and behavior".

Ann looked overwhelmed and at a loss for words. A woman of faith and strong convictions, Ann searched her heart for a response. "Well, I see. I know the center is known for their great work and the success of their clients", Ann said thoughtfully. Tamara was her only child and she wanted her to have the right influences in life. Here before her was a young man she had enjoyed the company of this evening and she had come to admire him; formed her opinion of without knowing this startling part of his pass. She had appraised him by his conduct in her house.

Was that enough? She asked herself. She didn't want to diminish this young man's victory over addiction and she certainly believed everyone is capable of being redeemed. She thought of Bible verse John 3:16-17 concerning God's plan for salvation: "For God so loved the world that he gave his one and only son, that whoever believes in him shall not perish but have eternal life. For God did not send his son into the world to condemn the world, but to save the world through him".

Ann let the Bible verse be her focus as she now looked at Manny and then at Tamara. "Okay, guys, let's discuss things further guided by God's wisdom", she gently informed them.

SARAH

Sarah walked slowly towards the intersection of Nehemiah and Frederick Douglass; it was a block away from Tamara's apartment building. She paused for a minute and looked around, unsure of exactly where she was. This was an unfamiliar neighborhood to her. She scanned the parked cars and looked at the brick buildings with bright lights in the window of the rooms dotting the front of the structures. She gazed for a while, thinking about the lives of the people in those rooms. Indistinct memories of her life with her husband, Edmond, swirled in her head. She tried to concentrate and slow the images down. She remembered his kind eyes looking at her, with a twinkle of mischief in them, as he teased her about her reactions to the many new experiences in their new home in Brooklyn. He was immensely delighted in her enjoyment of licking a cool cup of flavored shaved ice called icies that were sold from a street vendor's cart on the sidewalks in their neighborhood. A vision of Edmond holding onto her as they rode the biggest rollercoaster in Coney Island, tweaked the emerging memories of the past. He gripped her tightly, so she had no fear of using both of her hands to hold her headscarf in place to keep it from flying off as the rollercoaster dipped perilously through steep turns. The memory of the motions of the rollercoaster matched the swirling, fleeting sensations of visual glimpses of her past. Somewhere in there she felt a sudden unexplainable hurt. A memory of something smooth and cuddly that she used to embrace tenderly, peeked at her and then was gone. She looked at the surroundings again. Shuffling her feet, she moved on, stopping when she had crossed the intersection and reached the curb of the next sidewalk. Further up the street she saw three men standing close together, in dark hooded jackets whispering excitedly and glancing at the row of houses on the block with intense interest. Sarah continued towards them, and as they became aware of her approaching presence, they abruptly stopped talking and watched her closely. Their look was hostile, but Sarah had no need for fear; as awareness of her surroundings and their imposing potential for danger, hardly ever registered in her mind. She preceded with no fear. As she passed them, the men noted that she sung a soft melody interspersed with mumbling. Whatever their first apprehensions were about her, they now chuckled mockingly and condescendingly ignored her and went on with their whisperings. Sarah's steps were slow as she passed the men and then abruptly stopped and had an intense look of concentration on her face. "Who's there?" she questioned, peering at the shadows casted by the buildings around her that blocked the reflecting lights of the street light fixtures. "Who's there?", she called out again as she sensed the presence of entities she couldn't identify. She looked back at the three men. Her eyes watched as a grey haze moved over the small group of men. It's contour moved and formed an outline of some sort of beast. Sarah jerked in alarm and then the haze was gone. Had it really been there? Her mind grasped the possibility that she had indeed seen something

The men standing where the hazed had hovered over, were still engaged in their excited exchange, having forgotten Sarah's presence and did not act as if they had seen the haze that had formed above them. Sarah finally acknowledged their menacing persona, and shrinked involuntarily, acting purely on some ingrained instinct. Some voice prompted her to quickly leave the area, and she advanced up the street in a quickening shuffle, ten little steps for every normal step. She was determined to not look back. The least danger being that she might witness the grey haze hovering over the men again

As she hurried along with a new found energy, her voice rose in a clear high pitched soprano that vibrated intensely as she sung "Praise God, Praise God" over and over, then dropped down to mezzo-soprano echoing "Praise God" in that range. Going even lower, she then sung in the Contralto range the same worship of "Praise God", no longer mumbling. The three men did not hear her as she had now covered some distance away from them. Her steps taking her further away from the men, now seem to match the rhythm of her singing. From windows some residents of the surrounding buildings looked to see who was singing so loudly and beautifully. Sarah moved away from the neighborhood unaware of them, only of her song. The music of Sarah's vocal instrument filled the night air and without her being aware of her steps and surroundings, Sarah, immersed in her profound worship of God, walked into Calvary Zion Church, located a half a mile from Tamara's apartment building. It was only when she had stepped into the foyer of the church that she became conscious of where she was. Blinking her eyes, she studied the people who sat in the sanctuary in row upon row of what looked like a great multitude of worshipers. The heads of some of the individuals seated turned around and looked back at Sarah as she approached the open door to the inner room. Sarah was instantly startled as some of the faces peering at her resembled some of her favorite singers of all times. Comforted by the smiling faces looking intensely at her. Sarah shyly walked forward to a back row and sat down.

THE FIRE

The mess hall of Fire Station 29 was dimly lit and a few firefighters were sitting at various tables, either eating or finishing up their evening meal. Joe Billings, the Fire Chief, had moments ago walked through the hall acknowledging the guys with small banter and words of praise for the Firefighters' tireless efforts these past weeks in diligently working together as a team, handling extreme challenges that left all exhausted but still committed in ensuring the safety of the City's citizens as well as their homes. There had been a brief pause in the frequency of the recent fires; bringing about some relief and hope that the worst was over; that things would go back to a normal routine, with only an occasional fire sporadically. The guys enjoyed the break and were more relaxed and anticipated a festive holiday and fun times during rounds to friends and family; eating wonderfully cooked meals while they gathered in front of the T.V. watching Football, betting on which teams would make it to the playoffs; their wives sometimes joining them. Football, like other sports traditionally enjoyed by the men Folks, while seemingly ignored by females, had now been a shared experience for the whole family. Young kids also were enjoying the games; begging their parents to buy the sweat shirts with the number embroidered on them, of their favorite players. Gene Pendarous's sons argued constantly over their Football idols while Peter Menassah's girls were mesmerized by the superb shooting of various women players of the USA Basketball Women's National Team. All in all, everyone felt the approaching Holiday Season would be spectacular with all the games that would be played by some of the most outstanding players in the World,

Outside the Fire Station, the temperature was slowly dropping and there was the possibility that there might be some snow; as reported by the weather men and women of the local T.V. stations. Everyone in the Fire Station, as also the majority of the City's citizens were hoping the forecasted snow would not be a winter storm (even though this had not been forecasted, but everyone knows sometimes the weather predictions are off and occasionally, way off). Most of the forecast said to expect snow flurries, but Kenny, the new, recently hired fireman reminded the guys of the severe snowquail of 1970 that turned into a Winter Storm, closing down most of the City for well over seven days. Ben, the oldest firefighter among the guys, said he remembered that one.

"Hell, that was a monster. The snow was like packed ice, heavy and back breaking to clear off the sidewalks and my driveway stayed covered for days. I was just too exhausted to keep clearing the snow as it keep snowing continuously", Ben groaned as he remembered that snow event. The others in the mess hall had various remembrance of that Winter Snow. Most of the guys were too young to have experienced it, but there were a few near Ben's age, who could recall it.

It had been considered one of the most horrendous, deadly

winter storm in decades, or tens of decades. Ben's description of the impact it had, especially in New York was indeed very accurate. The sanitation department was overloaded with the vast job of clearing all the streets and highways. Schools were suspended for quite a few days; the young kids were delighted to be able to spend time outside with their friends and they welcomed participating in neighborhood against neighborhood snow fights. At the Johnson Projects, in East Harlem, the kids donned winter jackets and coats, along with putting on winter boots, gloves and heavy sweaters, and proceeded to march across Park Avenue to confront the kids from the Taft Projects that was the light Tan Brick Projects next to the Johnson Projects. The young kids on the lower East side around avenue A, in Manhatten in what is called Alphabet City, also were enjoying fantastic snow battles against each other. Most of the larger stores were closed and only a few local stores, where the proprietors who lived within the stores' building were open to meet the needs of the citizens of New York. Yes, it had been a rough time in most of the Eastern Coast line, affecting not only New York, but cities up from Georgia and tapering off near Maine, up north. There were some effects of the storm also in the mid Western States. Some people stated it seem as if God was fill of fury and simmering with vengeance over the actions of mankind. Churches were not able to meet during this time, the days stretched into endless hours because the Electrical Power was also knocked out in many areas forcing a strain on the workers who were trying to get electricity up and running again. Yes, hard times was felt that season.

Now in the mess hall the talk returned to the present. Joe

Billings returned to get a second cup of coffee and checked the time on the Wall Clock in the kitchenette. Before his eyes could focus on the time, the loud shrill blast of the Fire Station alarm resonated throughout the building. Billings forgot to look at the clock and headed back into the mess hall shouting,

"All right, guys let's move it; Pronto".

Everyone moved as one unit, focusing on getting geared up and into the Fire Trucks. With every one loaded on two trucks, the Fire Engines roared out of the Station and onto Schenectady Drive, racing towards middle Williamsburg, the destination Wassail Street and Liberty. The route to the fire took many turns as some of the streets were now being cleared of the freshly fallen snow that had finally arrived. Things were delayed somewhat because of this but when the trucks finally arrived they saw a blaze that engulfed most of the upper floors, probably where the fire originated Chief Billings speculated as he jumped off the first truck and started directing his crew of firefighters in a coordinated, plan approach to tackle the fire that now had aroused most of the building's occupants out of their beds and out of their apartments when they realized that their lives were in peril as the smoke from the upper floors drifted down and throughout all the hallways of the building. Tamara and her mother Ann were among the first to leave the building and huddled outside with the increasing crowd of tenants who watched anxiously the spreading and destruction of the flames engulfing their home. Many wondered if the building would withstand the intense heat and burn of the roaring fire.

The firemen raced up the stairway, bumping into fleeing apartment dwellers as they fled from the building, many bringing along their most treasured possessions that they were able to carry along with them. Tamara and Ann both looked at the same time and saw Raul laboring with halting steps to cross the street with his arms tightly holding a number of Braille Christian Devotionals and his prized large copy of the New King James Bible. Tamara rushed over and offering to help him, told him she would carry some of the books. At first he didn't want to relinquish any of them but finally allowed her to carry a few while he insisted that he had to carry his large Bible; he said it's burden was not heavy. Tamara smiled in wonderment at his statement and gently held his books for him while guiding him towards her mother standing far away from the sidewalk edge.

Meanwhile, Nettie on the fourth floor was still in the building trying to get her young kids into their coats and gloves as she urgently shouted at her mother Louise to look for her youngest son who she couldn't locate among her children. Louise rushed through the apartment calling Jeremy's name (he was named Jeremiah after the prophet from the Old Testament of the Holy Bible and like the prophet, little Jeremy was often in danger). Louise was now quite frighten as she looked in all the bedrooms and had not found him. Her heart racing, she tried to breathe slowly. The smoke was starting to fill the apartment and she had seen flames in the back, last bedroom. Saying the Lord's Prayer as she had learnt it as a child, she felt a calmness come over her and she remembered little Jeremy's favorite hiding place, her bedroom's closet. She now raced there and found Jeremy sleeping, curled up with his little action figure doll she had given him last year for his birthday. His eyes were peacefully closed and his arms hugged his doll and her crochet blanket that she had made him. Gently she reached down and picked him up and hushed his whimpering when he became aware of his nap being interrupted. Quickly she walked into the hall to only find out that the exit that way was now blocked by flames that were burning the carpet and bundle of bags there that were suppose to be given as a donation at the neighborhood church. She quickly backed up and reentered her bedroom.

"Nettie take the other kids outside quickly. The apartment is now on fire" she yelled to her daughter. "I will try to wait in my room for the firemen. I have Jeremy. Tell the firefighters to try to reach us from below my window."

"Oh my God, Mom, please don't worry. I am leaving now to get help". Nettie responded and rushed out the apartment with her kids, yelling as she went to the firemen in the hallway; she tried to explain the situation to them.

Below on the third floor Kwuame heard her cries and raced up the stairs to help her carry her children, with the help of a fireman, to safety outside. He and the fireman raced back upstairs. The fireman told him he should leave now but Kwuame refused to leave and raced back into Nettie's apartment calling out to Louise; meanwhile the firefighter helped the Lopez family leave the burning building. Joshua Rosenshein and Shannah were in the hallway and heard Kwuame's scream. Joshua urged Shannah to leave without him because he said he must help Kwuame. Frightened she agreed to leave. Joshua now hurried into the burning apartment and saw that Kwuame had fallen from the smoke and heat, and laid unconscious on the floor. He reached down and with some struggling, he managed to pick Kwuame up and inch by inch, made it to the apartment opened door. The flames were now blocking the exit from the door, it was directly burning in front of the door, and from the rug it had advanced further into the hallway, which had now also become a location filled with the heat and choking smoke The firefighter must have gone below to the other floors and Joshua in a panic raced to the kitchen, laid Kwuame down and he gathered and soaked as many kitchen towels as he could find and laid them on Kwuame's face and upper body, then with renewed strength he raced out into the hallway. The flames strung his arms and whole body placing him in intense agony as he tried to prevent his mind from acknowledging the physical torture of pain radiating all over him. With an impossible strength, he pushed forward and without a sense of time or any awareness where he was, he managed to reach the stairs and somehow descended step by step till he reached the third floor, then the second floor and finally arrived at the first floor and somehow was now finally at the building's large front doors leading outside. Trembling, weak and finally registering all the pain and weakness in his body he advanced forward and exited into the welcomed cool night air and through scorched lungs took labored breaths. Two firefighters outside saw him with Kwuame and raced forward and grabbed Kwuame from his weak arms and then one fireman from the second truck rushed to Joshua and helped him lower himself onto the sidewalk. There were now ambulances on the scene and paramedic workers placed him onto a stretcher and picked it up, then raced with urgency to a waiting ambulance and lifting the stretcher put him inside and climbed inside with him and closed the door. With sirens wailing they took off; traveling at max speed they raced to the nearest hospital with their patient.

Back at the fire location, the other tenants watched as the many firemen were trying to reach Louise, who was now at her bedroom window. She was yelling for them to catch her grandson and told them she would have to drop him out of the window because the bedroom was now engulfed with flames. Groups of firemen and tenants gathered as a rescue trampoline was placed below Louise's bedroom window's position on the east side of the building. Everyone shouted for her to drop little Jeremy to the waiting crowd and trampoline below. With fear and prayers, Louis released Jeremy from her arms and watched as he fell, as in slow motion. With joy she couldn't contain, Louise said "Amen" as she saw Jeremy safely fall onto the trampoline then scooped up by a fireman. The crowd now told her to jump; and struggling she climbed up onto the windowsill and placed one foot out to jump but the other foot got caught and losing her balance she fell directly to the left of the trampoline and hit the pavement. The crowd of tenants, firefighters, ambulance workers and neighboring residents from the various close by buildings screamed in unison at the horror of Louise's broken body on the sidewalk. No one could move for sometime, before finally they all seemed to awaken at the same time and activity resumed.

FIRE AFTERMATH

Nettie held little Jeremy tightly and the other three other children gathered closely next to her, also wanting her embrace. Soon the crowd standing around them moved aside as another ambulance arrived and the paramedics came forward and gently lifted Louise's body slowly after they had covered it with a blanket. They told Nettie where her mother's body would be taken (to Springfield Memorial Hospital Morgue) where Nettie could go later to have her mother transfer to a funeral home. Nettie listened and thanked them. A police officer approached and kindly told her that he and his partner would give her a ride to the Blue Cross Shelter, where the other tenants were being taken; who like her, were now homeless. With a heavy sigh, Nettie coaxed her kids forward and followed the officer.

Tamara and Ann with Raul got into Ann's car and also made the journey several city blocks away to the Blue Cross Shelter after being given the directions by Sergeant Braithwaite, who stood at the intersection of Nehemiah and Wassail, giving assurance and words of comfort to the distressed occupants of 101 Wassail Avenue, the completely demolished burnt shell of their former home. Shannah Rosenshein had already left, traveling in her Blue

Ford Windstar SUV, behind the ambulance that had taken her husband to Springfield Memorial Hospital.

Kwuame had regained consciousness an hour earlier and had assured the paramedics, after they had examined him thoroughly, that he could get a ride with his parents, who stood by, anxiously watching him, Mr and Mrs. Haynes hugged Kwuame before the three of them walked up the block to where Mr. Henry Haynes had his vintage 1975 Silver Cadillac Eldorado, his pride and joy, that he had for twenty years already. Kwuame marvelled all the time, how like a newly purchased car it looked. Mr. Haynes practically worshipped that car, spending many hours of his free time on the weekends, polishing and vacuuming it religiously, noticing any disturbances to it's appearance. Now the three Haynes settled into the car's interior, exhausted and tired; slowly they left the block and also headed to the hospital.

"Dad, did you say that it was Mr. Rosenshein, our neighbor on the third floor who rescued me from Nettie's apartment?" Kwuame asked his Father.

"Yes, son. Your mom and I thought you had left the building when we saw you dash into the hallway. We didn't hear Nettie yelling, but obviously you heard her. Anyway when we arrived outside and looked for you, we couldn't find you. Then soon Nettie came out and told us what happened. We all soon saw Mr. Rosenshein carry you out and you were unconscious. Poor man. I believe he has sustained some serious injuries and burns. Thank God for his bravery son. You are alive because of him".

Kwuame looked bewildered and astonished at the information his father had given him. "Why" He asked himself "Why would that old Jewish man risk his life to help me?" Kwuame believed that someone had said Mr. Rosenshein had cancer, which made it even more amazing that he would even attempt to rescue Kwuame and then to succeed. Truly amazing, Kwuame contemplated, as he watched the passing buildings flash by as his father's car drove up Broadway Avenue. The passing scenery from the car window really didn't register to his conscious mind; he was lost in thoughts about his many reservations towards Jews and Whites that seem to increase exponentially daily, each year. He thought of the many examples he felt demonstrated a lack of concern for the plight or injustice suffered by the Black Race over the many years by the white race. Hell, he thought, centuries. He felt history confirmed this fact. He thought of the years slavery had been allowed to exist. The hardships suffered by his people even after slavery was supposed to have been abolished over two hundred years ago. What about the rape of Black Women by White Men during all those years of slavery and the audacity of the White Man to hang Black Men for having sex with White Women; in some cases, quite a few, it wasn't even rape, just a lie to kill a Black Man. He remembered the tale of the young boy, Emmitt Till, who was killed back in Mississippi, sometime around 1955. He was only fourteen years old and only was accused of offending a White Woman by making a childish, innocent remark to her after being dared by his friends to talk to her. Kwuame breathed slowly, trying to not get mad over his reflections and thought again of Mr. Rosenshein's actions tonight.

Kwuame finally realized they had arrived at the hospital. Mr. Haynes' Eldorado pulled into a parking space at the hospital's main parking area and as they all climbed out of the car, Kwuame saw that his mom was carrying his flute.

"Glee, mom you retrieved my flute from the apartment". He wrapped his mom in a tender embrace, then hugged her tightly.

"Oh, thank you so much mom".

"That's okay son. I know how much this flute means to you and since your uncle Khaaliq gave it to you as a gift, I didn't want you to lose it in the fire. I know that it means the world to you, like that shiny car of your father's means to him". She smiled broadly and then laughed happily in spite of the dismal circumstances of the evening and the coming prospect of a uncertain future. They all entered the hospital's emergency room and waited with the other people to be seen by the doctors on duty.

Shannah, now had some fellow worshipers from her synagogue surrounding her in the waiting room, who had responded to her telephone calls for their support and prayers. The group was small but their prayers were intense as they prayed non-stop for God's mercy and protection of Joshua. Few others from the apartment were there; most, had been able to get out of the building without suffering more than severe cases of smoke inhalation. The ones who were present still were in shock over Louise's death and their own predicament of now being homeless. Some hospital staff spoke of some of the services in place, that offered aid and assistance to the homeless. They were given a printed list of their services with their address and telephone numbers.

Meanwhile across town at the Blue Cross Shelter, Tamara and Ann, along with Raul, were sitting in a group surrounding Nettie and her kids as they all listened to the shelter workers assign the sleeping areas for everyone and dispense toilettes and blankets. They were told that they would receive additional services offered to them tomorrow and a list of available service similiar to what the patients at Springfield Memorial Hospital received, offered by the city to the homeless.

"Mom, we are going to need new clothes. I can't go to school today in my pajamas",. Tamara moaned in a whisper to Ann.

"You don't have to go to school today, I'll call in sick later and we can go and shop at the Goodwill Store and pick out a few necessary things. Fortunately I have some savings. But I wonder how many of the people here at the shelter are capable financially of buying themselves clothes. Maybe the list of services that the workers here said they would distribute tomorrow will have a location where these people can get free clothes". Ann reflected quizzically as she looked around at the bleak surroundings of the shelter. The walls looked as if they had not been painted in years. The furnishings were minimal and flimsy in stability and appearance. The floor had faded, dull worn out tile on it, that definitively needed to be replaced. "My God" Ann thought "I had no idea these shelters were this depressing looking". She leaned closer to Tamara and hugged her, whispering,

"Don't worry honey, everything is going to turn out okay. We have to trust God to meet our needs and direct our lives according to his will. It's going to be okay; Don't worry" Ann's words were a comfort to Tamara and she decided then to let the situation be handled by God. She looked at all the other people filling this dismal haven that was their new haven their new home and the rough journey facing them and also herself and Tamara. How to manage working while also trying to find a new place to start over again; for her this was a new experience, the first time she faced such a giant; a swallowing large fish that she now was in the belly of. Like Jonah from the bible. She had not been running from any command from God, so why had he abandoned her and Tamara. They lingered in this situation, now homeless; no processions, no shelter but this squalid place; lacking beauty. The other residents looked like they also thought the same. She saw a little boy and girl, sitting nearby next to a woman who looked like she was drunk, her head bobbing forward and back; Ann thought "maybe she is high, not drunk". The little boy and girl sat silently looking lost, hardly even noticing each other. Ann wanted to cry at the hopless, shabby, unkempt look of these precious little lost sheep, in need of a parental shepard but instead had the poorly equipped quidance of this forlon lost creature; their mother who obviously was probably strung out on drugs. Ann silently prayed for this little family, and tried to plan her actions for today; the call she had to make to her job, the trip that she and Tamara needed to make today to get clothes for themselves.

"Come on Tamara honey. Let us go lay down for a while and try to get some sleep".

"Okay, mom. I am tired and I do want to lay down for awhile" Tamara agreed and got up and with a heavy heart, followed Ann to their designated sleeping area and bent over the green cot that had sheets and a blanket for it. She followed her mother's example and spread the bedding across the cot and then sunk down and tried to get a few hours of sleep.

TAMARA'S JOURNAL ENTRY

It seems a lifetime ago that I started this journal; so full of excitement and energy, wanting to do an excellent job of presenting the thoughts of a young black female teenager to the world. As it has turned out, something I didn't anticipated has occurred and has left me quite shaken and profoundly sadden and that has impacted my life tremendously and brought some of the issues, that I had discussed in my initial journal entry, home; dead center into my life; for one, my mother and I have become homeless. We have become one of the statistics that you read about or hear of on the evening news on television. We lost everything. Our beautiful apartment was totally demolished; everything that we have poured into it to make it our home was lost within a matter of a few hours. All our creative energy that went towards making it a secure haven against all outside forces was in the end equated to a hollow and futile effort; we were left with nothing.

What was it that caused such devastation so quickly? It was none other than that physical force that has been around since the dawning of time; Fire. The same force that God probably utilized in creating the cosmo; look at the stars which are basically heated gases and fire. This same force that God created also destroys.

When the Bible speaks about God's wrath in the end destroying everything by fire, I can well imagine it.

When we stood outside on the sidewalk across the street from our apartment building looking at the roaring fire being fought by the firefighters, our initial feelings were of immense relief because we had gotten out alive. As we continued watching and the cold air finally penetrated our numb minds, we were reminded that we only had on our night gowns under our winter coats and whatever we could find to put on our feet; slippers on mom's feet and sneakers on mines. All other clothing that we owned we soon realized was being burned in that scorching inferno that stood before us. We both were angry about losing all our personal belongings and treasures. Some were little inexpensive items costing next to nothing like the little delicate glass table mom had brought me for my bedroom. She had found it at a state fair in Virgina a few years ago on one of our summer visits to see her parents. I loved that little table. I remember vividly the day mom brought it; Fairs were always my passion. I loved walking around smelling the various aromas and seeing the many sights that would take me on a sensory odyssey. The fluffy pink cotton candy blowing in the air and the crisp, taut smell of barbecue chicken mixed with cooked sausage and onions; the loud crowds, sensations that made me truly happy. That day I was more happy and excited than ever. I was going with my mom and grandparents to the Garden EXpo State Fair and was going to present my own home grown tomatoes that grandma had helped me plant in her garden at the beginning of the summer. I was certain my ripe succulent shiny tomatoes the size of little mellons would take first place. I couldn't wait to show my anticipated winning ribbon to my classmates in September. I didn't win, but to help ease my disappointment, mom brought me the table.

It was a combination magazine holder and picture stand (one more of my passions). In the magazine section I had placed a few magazines and also snuck in some of my record collection - Whitney, Gerald Lavert, Boys to Men, and also James Cleveland that Ginny had given me. On top of the glass table were lined up my collection of pictures of family and friends; now lost forever, was one of Ginny, Manny and I, taken in front of my building.

Our anger quickly turned to fear and the greatest sadness I have ever experienced. Louise, the grandmother of four young children, jumped to her death trying to escape the flames of the fire, after she had successfully saved the life of her youngest grandchild, Jeremy, by throwing him out of the window to the trampoline held by firefighters below her window. She wasn't able to save herself; when she attempted to jump to the trampoline she tripped on her way out the window and instead of landing directly down onto the trampoline, she fell to the pavement to the left of it. We all watched in horror at her body hitting the hard cement ground. I felt a sickness indescribable. Louise's poor daughter and grandchildren were devastated and cried mournfully.

FIRE AND DEMONS

The gathering of arsonists were present in their meeting place the next day after the fire and also among them were again a legion of demons smirking with glee at all they had managed to succeed in doing through their manipulation of this group of arsonists. They had a worldwide network of arsonists and angry people they were controlling masterfully. The arsonists, unaware of the various games that they were an intricate function of and a source of amusement, congratulated each other for destroying another apartment building complex that was owned by rich profiteers. A bellicose assortment of lower rank demons were making the most noise while proudly placing themselves nearest to the arsonists, demanding a place of importance to the demonic cause set up by the head demon, Abaddon. Abaddon, floating above everyone, chuckled at the mischievous, loud, lower rank demons. To him everyone was of a lower rank; he would not allow this to be challenged, placing any demon who dared to try to outrank him, quickly in place with a sharp piercing of their torso, inflicted by his sharp talons, which were gruesome to look at. They were four feet long and filled with ridges that were formed by layers upon layers of hard Keratin protein, that he proudly displayed by waving them constantly as he spoke or gave instructions to the mass of legions of demons under his command.

While the humans had gathered around the body of Louise as she laid motionless, crumbled by her fall; Abaddon did not feel the ultimate satisfaction of other kills he had orchestrated, because this mortal one would not enter his underworld. No, Louise would be destined to the Kingdom of his enemy, the pompous Creator, the "I Am" of the 360 names, representing many attributes mentioned in the bible; the circle of life. Abaddon huffed in fury at the thought of the "Almighty" and his band of angels and pathetic saints; all losers. In his fury he had circled the room 100 times at the speed of sound before he was able to regain his equilibrium and slowed down and came to his original position, centered above the arsonists and his legion of demons. Just then he heard one of his demons who sounded like he felt that maybe they, the demons, should not contend with men and just let them destroy themselves.

Swiftly Abaddon rushed to confront the demon.

"Who are you? Are you an imposter? An angel among our ranks?" He hissed in rage at a silvery, hovering demon, who as he carefully looked him over, slowly took on the form of one of the Creator's angels and who suddenly exposed a luminous set of feathery wings that extended from behind his shoulder blades.

Outraged that an anglel had the audacity to enter Abaddon's horde of demons and to further try to sway them to righteousness, he lashed out in a deadly, precise infliction of his four feet talons across the fake demon's silvery face, that in it's now appearance of Beauty, sicken Abaddon.

"Kill him, kill him, immediately. He is one of the Almighty's disgusting angels" He roared with hatred, seething in madness that twisted his face to its present grotesque appearance. The other demons jerked back in a defensive stance, as if they might be lashed out at by Abaddon; then quickly remembered that they were his army who were called to be obedient to him and rushed forward to attack the angel among them. With a speed that shocked them, the angel flew out an open window and completely vanished from sight. Astounded, the demons questioned this feat; how was it possible? Was this fleeing angel the archangel Michael: Protected by the Almighty, the "I Am"? Abaddon also did not grasp the possibility of such a miracle to have happened in his domain. The angel must have been divinely protected. Disgusted he told his troops to concentrate on the humans, after all they were the weak ones of God's Kingdom, without the strength and wisdom of God's angels. "Why did God care so much for them? They care only for themselves. They do not mourn for others. They have watched me strike down all their prophets and saints for centuries and do not lift a hand to prevent this. It has been so easy to get them to hate each other Look how magnificiently I was able to kill their savior. Oh how joyfully I celebrated at their stupidity and foolish pride. They killed their only chance for salvation." Abaddon then remembered the purpose of God for this occurrence; this slaughter of God's son. The promise of salvation for any who would call upon the savior's name and be baptized by it and the name of the father, God, and the Holy Spirit. Again Abaddon felt intense hate and the pride that plagued him for eons, filled his being once again with his eternal jealousy towards God.

"I must return to controlling the Humans" He said with

renewed emphasis and swooped down among his lower demons feeling an renewed power among his inferiors; the other demons and of cause, the weaklings; men. He took his place hovering over the arsonists in the great meeting hall.

Below, the "Lion" was once again controlling the audience by some unseen magnetism that he possessed. Few people are able to wedge control of multitudes of people with up most authority. Hitler had had this ability. Whether it had served him well though, is questionable in the least assessment of the man. He had power and probably some wealth, but it was a costly affair; with hate felt toward him no matter where he went. But the "LION had yet to experience such a tremendous price. His life at his conception he felt was a destined one. He was an immortal. He really believed this. The universe made special preparation for his entrance. His mother had assured him of this from infancy, as she whispered constantly "our Lord and savior". His countrymen also took up this chant as they watched him grow from boyhood to his magnificent physical statue.

Posing, with pride, the Lion declared,

"It will soon be completed. Be patient, my brothers. The wealth mongers of the world will be under our thumbs very soon." Few in the audience, who heard these words were aware of the Lion's own wealth (an estimated one hundred Billion in U.S. currency), a wealth hidden from his followers. Many actually believed he led an austere existence, lacking any lavish comforts, while in reality, not known to them, he had many residents; homes located all over the world, in many countries. Not even high ranked members of the Brotherhood were aware of this.

SHANNAH

Five days had past since the fire and Shannah had left the hospital only once when fellow synagogue friends had encouraged her to join them at their homes to wash and freshen herself and change clothes and now she sat near Joshua's bed and as in the other previous nights, sponged his forehead and face with a wet cloth, touching only the areas not bandaged up. He looked feverish and she worried about the latest report of the attending doctors that he was in extreme danger of hypovolemic shock. He had a Staphylocci infection now. He had required fluid resuscitation on the second day of hospitalization. The nurses regularly cleaned and debrided his blisters, removing dead skin, applied topical antibacterials and wound dressing and a constant flow of I.V. opiates were administered around the clock. He came in and out of consciousness, calling out her name softly. Today, earlier in the afternoon, he managed a brief conversation with her and his sons when they were here. The sons had left for the day and Shannah felt so alone watching the man she had loved so dearly for so many years as he now battled for his life; for the second time. "Why God, why so much testing and physical challenges for this man?", she questioned God, in sorrow. Hadn't he been faithful in his obedience to all your commands, He is a good man. Must he continuously face these trials?" Almost immediately Shannah felt ashamed of daring to interrogate the Creator. To bring before him a wife's plea for mercy for her mate; her beloved Joshua. To dare to criticize the maker of Heaven and Earth. She lowered her head and broke out into a feverish recitation of the Priestly Blessing from the Bible's Old Testament, the book of Numbers, chapter six, verse 24-26,

"The Lord Bless you and keep you;

The Lord make his face shine upon you

and be gracious to you;

The Lord turn his face toward you

and give you peace".

She hung unto the prayer and repeated it several times until she lost track of her words and looked up and saw Kwuame standing in the doorway.

"Goodness, Kwuame, Thank you for coming, please come in", Shannah said with joy at the prospect of company during her loneliness.

"Hello, Mrs Rosenshein. Are you sure you don't mind me interrupting your time with your husband?" Kwuame said as he stepped into the room feeling awkward and nervous."

"No, I welcome your presence. Believe me, it is alright. Please sit down.", she indicated the other vacant chair in the room, a few feet from her.

Kwuame walked to it and eased down into it as if he might spring up suddenly and make a dash for the door.

"How is Mr Rosenshein?" What are the doctors telling you?" He questioned with hesitation.

"It is not good, Kwuame. He has a Staphylocci infection now and severe burns. Doctors have him on around the clock opiates". Shannah's voice caught at the word opiates. "It's effects has made Joshua incoherent most of the times when he is awake."

"He has to be watched carefully and his vital signs recorded numerous times during the day. He might not make it." she said.

"I am so sorry", Kwuame blurted out. "It is because of me that he is now hospitalized. Why did he risk coming upstairs to help me?" Kwuame asked in sorrowful confusion.

"Hush, Kwuame. It is not your fault. All that happens to us is governed by God. It is not for us to question why", Shanna said gently as she witness Kwuame's guilt written in his eyes.

"Do you know Joshua has sons?" she said.

"Yes, Mrs Rosenshein" Kwuame answered.

"Well then, Joshua will live on, no matter what the outcome is. Our boys are so much like him. It is as if God has put all Joshua's attributes in his sons. His gentleness, his laughter and joy of life. His talents and wisdom. And so much more." Shannah said with intense conviction.

Kwuame swallowed a lump in his throat.

"Do you have any extra pictures of him? I would like to remember him if he passes and the sacrifice he has made for me", Kwuame asked with equal intensity and urgency, not wanting to forget to make this request.

"Yes, I have many pictures of him and I am sure Joshua would like you to have one of them." Shannah's voice was kind and comforting in her lack of accusation of blame.

"But how about you, Kwuame. Did the fire burn you?"

"I have only suffered superficial burns. Really mainly small reddish blisters. They don't hurt. Thank you for asking, Mrs Rosenshein", Kwuame's voice quibbling as he said this.

"Good, good. But please, call me Shannah. That is my name. Please call me that." she gently urged Kwuame.

"Yes, Mrs....oh sorry, Shannah", Kwuame stumbled then laughed at himself.

"I see you and Mr. Joshua with your sons and little ones trodding along with you. Are those your grandchildren?"

"Yes, the little angels. I probably should say devils", Shannah laughed heartily.

"No, I know I shouldn't say that. They are really precious. Just so mischievous",. She again laughed merrily. Kwuame watched her and wondered at her ability to laugh at a time like this, with her husband practically entering death's doorway (pass the point of just knocking on it).

"I know what you mean. I have a friend named Nat and I must say that descriptive adjective would surely fit him too, even though he is the best friend I ever had". Kwuame was also now laughing.

Leaning forward, Kwuame then asked gently,

"Will you be alright if Joshua doesn't make it?"

Shannah looked into Kwuame's eyes and saw his kind concern there.

"Yes, I think so. But I am afraid I might not", she admitted

"He has been my world for most of my life. We met while he

attended a Yeshiva and I attended a nearby Seminary school a few blocks from his school. I think he liked me immediately" Shannah bragged.

"He would do the traditional boyish prank and pull my hair, while teasing me". Shannah looked ecstatic at the moment she mentioned this fond memory of her Joshua, the man she vowed to love for eternity more than once during the many years she and Joshua had spent together.

Kwuame watched the light in her eyes and felt a supreme agony that his rescue by her husband might be the eventual cause of the lost of light in her beautiful eyes. At that moment he realized the beauty present in those eyes. "Oh God, forgive my actions that might have been an unplan cause of the light going out of the eyes of innocence." He thought.

The day went on effortlessly creating a bond between Shannah and Kwuame; they talked about her Joshua and she questioned him about his family; the father who she saw on so many mornings polishing that classic shiny silver Eldorado, which obviously he admired as he scrubbed and polished it. He indeed took excellent care of it with a pride for its elegance and performance. The car's luster could be seen even from Shannah's window. And then she recognized his mother too, as she always hurried out of 101 Wassail Avenue with a bible in her hands. Shannah spoke to Kwuame about these observances now.

"Your mom and dad look like they have a good relationship. A happy marriage like me and my Joshua", she mentioned while smiling at the thought of another happy marriage, so rare with a lot of couples today, unfortunately.

"Yes, mom and dad have been together for many years. They dated for some years before they married. Like you and Mr. Rosenshein they meet at an early age. So yes, you can say they have a good relationship. They give a lot of advice about relationships, Maybe too much!!", Kwuame chuckled softly, thinking about the rule of his parents that didn't allow him to date before the age of sixteen. And their many inquires about the families of the girls he had dated.

"There is never too much advice that could be passed on by parents to their children". Shannah scolded lightly, in amusement at her husband's young visitor's words.

"No Mrs. Rosen...oh sorry, Shannah. I tell you the truth, they can be too involved with their help. I just want them to let me make my own decisions for myself. They treat me like a little toddler at times. You would think they might stick a pacifier in my mouth next!!!" Kwuame grinned widely in spite of his genuine annoyance of his parent's occasional restrictive interference.

"I look at you and you do not look to have suffered too much from parental interference; you seem to be a well balanced young man", Shannah voiced playfully.

"Every young man should be given, what appears to be excellent guidance", Shannah further remarked.

"Kwuame looked at her with faked frustration and then grinned.

"Okay, okay. I admit, my parents are great parents and are themselves full of wisdom. I also have to admit, I've benefited from most of their advice. I think they get some of their advice from the Bible. I don't attend church but they go and hardly miss any

Sunday service. I used to go, but haven't really lately. Maybe I will start again" Kwuame looked like he was again troubled, Shannah reflected and thought, "I must encourage him to not take on this weight of false blame for Joshua's condition."

"Kwuame, you do realize it is not your responsibility or fault for what has happened,, don't you? The cause of the fire is responsible for this tragedy of my Joshua, not you. Not you at all. Please realize that", Shannah softly said as she held Kwuame's gaze with her stare, looking intensively at him. Trying to make her point with clarity.

Kwuame had to direct his eyes from looking at her and turned as if he was examining the room. He wanted to forget the burden of the guilt he felt. He suddenly stood up and turned back to Shannah.

"Mrs. Rosen..., I'm sorry, I meant Shannah", he stumbled with his words.

"I have to go, but I will come back again if that is okay with you?", he inquired of Shannah.

"Most certainly, you are welcome at any time. Please, come anytime". She got up and walked with him to the door.

"Thank you, Kwuame for visiting and keeping me company today". Shannah quickly hugged Kwuame, surprising him and herself.

Kwuame walked down the hallway of the intensive care unit where Joshua's hospital room was located and again marveled at the sacrifice of Joshua in rescuing him from ultimate death had he remained unconscious in Nettie's apartment. He vowed that he would return to the hospital to see Joshua and hopefully be able to talk to him if he was awake. "I will thank him with sincere appreciation for what he has done", Kwuame thought and left the I.C.U area and arriving at the elevator, got on and descended to the main floor.

Back in Joshua's room, Shannah felt encouraged by the friendly company of Kwuame and reaching over she gasped Joshua's hand and whispered, "I love you, sweetie".

ANN AND TAMARA

Ann put the two Hundred Dollars she withdrew from the ATM machine into her wallet within her shoulder bag and turned to face Tamara.

"Come on sweetheart, let's see what we can pick up from the Good Will store. I've only taken out a small amount, I don't think I should spend too much. We are only going to get the bare necessities. Like three changes of underwear, one extra Bra, two pair of pants each, a sweater, three changes of shirts, and let me see, we will have to...you know, wait here. I think I might have to get another hundred dollars out of my saving account".

Ann turned abruptly and returned to the ATM machine and withdrew five twenty dollar bills and stuffed those into her purse and zipped up her shoulder bag. Returning to Tamara she quickly walked with her along the ten blocks to the nearby Goodwill store.

"Mom these clothes look really shabby. Can't we go somewhere else?" Tamara whined, looking at the rolls of hanging clothes on racks inside the store.

"Look honey, I know this situation is hard, but we are lucky to be alive. I mean we are blessed". Ann added. "We are going to have to make sacrifices".

"Okay, okay". Tamara answered in defeat and reluctantly walked along the racks of hanging second hand clothes. Suddenly she stopped and pulled a beautiful pink blouse from the middle of one roll of clothes. It was a size twelve; her size. She was pleased at her find and lifted up the blouse to show Ann

"Mom, look isn't this beautiful? Look at the fine details, the stitching along the neck and bodice". She exclaimed.

Ann smiled, pleased that Tamara had been able to find something that she really liked. Relief flooded her and she agreed with Tamara.

"The blouse is beautiful. Maybe I will be lucky too. Wait I see a light blue top that looks quite expensive. Wow, this is really great looking", Ann declared and held up the shirt she had found. Together, within one hour, Tamara and Ann were finished with their shopping and brought their selections to the cashier in the front of the store and watched her quickly ring up the total of all the clothes they had purchased. With satisfaction Ann saw that the total charge was two hundred and thirty five dollars. With the extra sixty five dollars, she had remaining she figured she could get essential toiletries later if the Blue Cross Homeless Shelter didn't supply them to the shelter's homeless. Walking back to the shelter, instead of taking the bus Ann decided would save them four dollars. Four dollars could be used to get coffee and a danish at the little coffee shop she had noticed earlier that was a short, close distance from the Shelter where they were staying at 1991 Sullivan Street. The coffee shop was at 1901 Sullivan Street and its name was Coffee and Sweets. She had noticed the shop's low prices displayed on it's clear glass window and on the store's placard that was stationed to the right side of the store's entrance.

"Sweetie, let's get some coffee. I saw a shop close by where we can go".

"Okay, mom, I'm on broad. I need some java in my body." Tamara laughed gaily.

"I think I'm going to buy a coffee pot and some coffee if they don't have those at the shelter", Ann considered.

Arriving at the coffee shop they were able to get seats at one of the tables located near the window. As Ann looked around she noticed a smooth skinned man looking at her. He had a mustache and was approximately five feet ten inches tall and watching his eyes she felt a sudden flutter in her stomach. She quickly turned away and looking at Tamara said,

"Gee, I really do need this pick up". The waitress arrived at that moment, and Ann turned to her,

"I'll have a cup of Carmel Frappucino Grande and also a Cheese Danish".

"Will that be all for you?" the waitress asked.

"Yes".

"What about you, what will you have?" she asked Tamara.

"I'll have a white chocolate Mocha Frappuccino and a Blueberry Bagel", Tamara said.

"Okay, I will have these for you all shortly", she said and walked away.

Tamara, then looked around and also noticed the smooth skinned man looking at her mother.

"Gee, mom. I think you have an admirer", she giggled.

"There is a handsome guy watching you. I mean he is really checking you out. And he is not bad looking".

"Stop. Tamara. Leave me alone. I am not interested. Forget him, please", she answered, frustrated and flattered at the same time. She glanced for a moment in the direction of the man acting as if she was only casually looking around again.

He looked into her eyes again and smiled broadly. Ann snapped her head away from his direction and nervously picked up her napkin. Then thought "What am I doing? This is ridiculous. I do not want to be bothered with any type of romance in my life. Not now. Why am I fluttered?"

Tamara was watching her and still giggling silently. In a few minutes the waitress brought their orders to them and they ate and talked.

"Do you realize mom, we will not be able to move back into 101 Wassail Avenue? The building is totally demolished." Tamara moaned.

"Yes, I have thought about that and again thank goodness that I have some savings. We will have to start looking immediately for a new apartment and some furniture. The Good Will store has some moderately priced items that we can get. Also I know that there are some organizations that have donations given to them by wealthy people, where we can get some things free without having to pay for them. Wow, I wished I had remembered earlier", Ann sighed.

"But I guess getting the things immediately that we purchased was essential. We needed a change of outfits to be presentable", she added. Ann and Tamara continued talking, while the smooth skinned man keep his eyes on Ann. Finally ready to leave, Ann went to pay for their meal. At the cashier, Ann dropped her money while trying to withdraw it out of her wallet. A hand covered hers as she picked up her money.

"Can I help you pick up your cash?" came a man's smooth baritone voice. Ann stared into the smooth skinned man's eyes, which were focused directly into her's, his face leveled with hers. Ann gulped and swallowed.

"It is alright, I can get it, thank you".

"Everyone needs help at times. You shouldn't resist help offered", he said playfully and reached to pick up some pennies and handed them to her.

"Thank you", Ann said, while thinking "if a man offers you pennies and their your own pennies, is that a good sign?." She straighten up and proceeded to finish paying for her meal and the man quickly walked beside her as she walked back to Tamara.

"Is it possible for me to get your name and number?" he asked.

"My name is Ann, but I don't give out my number to strangers."

"Well I come here in the evening after work and perhaps we can move beyond being strangers". He handed her his business card. It stated that he was a community activist and Director of a Community Organization called "Change our World". It stated that it wanted to promote racial harmony and community developement. Ann looked at him and said good-by and reaching Tamara, walked with her out the door.

"Who is he? I saw him give you his card."

"His name is Tony. A Tony Dawson the card stated".

"Are you going to call him?"

"No, leave me alone".

"Then why did you keep his card and not return it to him?" Tamara teased, linking her arm through Ann's. Together they walked slowly along as they observed their new neighborhood and reflected on all that had happened to them. While Tamara did most of the talking, Ann listened and found herself still at a lost of what the next few months ahead of them would bring. She looked at Tamara and again saw the faint and steadily emerging young woman she was becoming. "God, we shouldn't be in this predicament, what started the fire?" she asked herself. No one had given them any information yet about the cause of the fire. The news on television mentioned it might have been another instance of the handy work of the recent arsonists. She also thought again of the story of Jonah from the bible. Was she guilty of some sort of rebellion to God's directive like Jonah, the prophet? Had she failed to do something? The answer did not come to her and she refocused on what Tamara was saying.

RAUL

"Mr Vasquez, how are you doing?" Is there anyone you would like to call concerning your homelessness?" A member of the Blue Cross Shelter inquired of Raul. He was in the dayroom of the center. Ms. Cheryl Turner settled down on the sofa next to him and offered him a cup of coffee. He gladly took it from her and said,

"Thank you, Miss. I would like to cancel my group therapy class at the Genesis Awakement Center. If I could be shown to a phone, it would be appreciated".

"Most certainly. But are you a therapist there or a client?"

"I am one of their group therapist. I will need to make arrangements to get someone else for the clients and to be honest I need to find out where I can get another apartment". Raul shook his head in acknowledging his new circumstances.

"Well it is one of the things we will try to help you with during your stay here. Would you like our assistance, Mr Vasquez

"Yes, I guess that would be best."

"We are one of the only few organizations that provides direct help in getting our occupants the help they need to locate rental apartments", Ms. Turner informed Raul.

"We have a housing support worker who has compiled a list of available housing units, ready for rent, across the city. He updates the list daily, noting which units are no longer available for rent. We might have to hire an auxiliary person to work with him. The job is getting quite cumbersome for one person." She went on.

"I will speak with him today and have him sit down with you and get feedback from you of where you might want to live. Again units are opening up weekly".

Raul listened and tried to retain the information she was giving him but was half preoccupied with thoughts about the young people of his therapy group, more concerned about them. Some of them were at a fragile position in their lives. Many were from broken homes that were at poverty level, most without fathers to lead the family. Raul felt anxious about having to work rapidly to return to guiding them. He refocused his mind on what Ms. Turner was saying.

"We also can get you an application for Section Eight, it is a program you probably are aware of from working as a counselor".

"Yes, I am familiar with it. I know it gives subsidy to help you pay rent", he said.

"Yes, but unfortunately there is about a two years waiting time to receive it, if you qualify", Ms Turner interjected wistfully.

"But there is also what is called project based vouchers, PBV's. Money is available, supplementing the thirty percent of your income with monetary vouchers for the rest of the money for your housing".

"Well I wouldn't mind help with my rent. I hadn't heard about this program".

"Yes it is available through Public Housing Agencies or Authorities. We provide help in getting you in touch with them".

"Miss Turner, is there any religious services offered here at the center?"

"No, I am sorry, with so many diverse religious affiliations it would be hard to provide them all".

"That is true, I suppose. I belong to a church that welcomes all denominations, all religions. I was baptized there". Raul said with pride.

"My blind eyes were opened to God's plan for his children; unity. My church is a Christian church that preaches the Gospel of Jesus Christ which offers salvation to all".

"Mr Vasquez, what is the name of your church?" Ms Turner smiled and asked.

"It is Broken Lives Tabernacle, located within walking distance of my former neighborhood".

"Will you want to attend services this weekend?"

"Yes, I would like to. Again I would need to make a phone call for a ride to church this Sunday also. I forgot to take my phone when the fire started and left without it", he explained.

"Great, I can help you with making those calls. Would that be okay?"

"yes, certainly, thank you".

"Do you want to make the calls now. I have a phone available in my office".

"Yes, thank you again, Ms. Turner".

"Do you want me to hold your arm and guide you to my office?

"That is very kind of you. Yes, I would appreciate that". Cheryl Turner hooked her arm under Raul's arm and together they made their way across the floor of the dayroom to the hallway leading to the administrative offices of the shelter. At the rear of the hallway Ms Turner stopped and taking her keys she opened the door of her office. Carefully she helped Raul to her desk and pulled a chair over towards him and asked him to please sit down. Slowly Raul lowered himself into the seat. Cheryl moved her Samsung :3105 phone towards him.

"Can I dial the numbers for you?"

"Yes, please", Raul gave her the number of his job and she quickly dialed it for him and handed the phone to him. Telling him she would be back in a few minutes she left the office. Raul listened to the phone ringing and then the center's receptionist voice came through.

"Hello, this is the Genesis Awakement Center. How can I help you?"

"Good day, Alisha, this is Raul".

"Hello, Raul. Gee I'm sorry, I heard about the fire in your apartment Building. How are you?"

"Well, in spite of the chaos of being displaced and now homeless, I am trying to hang in there". Raul told her, appreciative of her concern.

"Could you inform Mr. Solomon, who handles scheduling, that I will have to take some time off, it might be a while. He will need to arrange for another therapist to take my position in group therapy. Also I left some materials on my office desk, it is music for Christmas. Could you get it to Ruby, from my group. She loves singing and I wanted her to have these CD's. Also I am trying to get a ride to church. I plan on calling my church for that, but if anyone else could help out in the future, I would appreciate the help. I will text you my current address, alright?"

"Sure, no problem Raul. I will get started on this right away".

"Again, thank you so much Alisha, take care. Hope to be back soon. Good-bye."

"Good-bye, Raul, you take care too".

They both hung up their phones. Raul then slowly tried to dial the other number he needed to call. He thought to himself, "When are they going to make voice activated phones for the Blind and other handicap people?" The phone again ringed after a few brief seconds. Another familiar voice answered the call.

"Hello, who is calling?" his church member, Teddy asked.

"Hi, Teddy, this is Raul".

"Hey Raul, man, that is tragic what has happened to you guys. The fire's destruction was shown on T.V. How are you? And where are you?"

"I am at the Blue Cross Shelter on 1991 Sullivan Street", Raul said, and then said, after a pause,

"It is kinda of tough, to be honest. I am trying to get my bearings. The process of adjusting to this new circumstance is challenging", he again stopped.

"I am learning to gain perseverance, that is one of the lessons taught by the staff of therapists at the center. I now realize that it is a lesson that comes over and over again in our lives. A process, perhaps, of repetition that God uses to strengthen and mold us", he said to Teddy.

Teddy was Raul's most appreciated friend in his life, having known him for many years, during which a bond of sharing ideas and interests had flourished steadily and developed into a solid foundation of support for each other. Teddy was a writer, he had published various works of poetry and non-fiction books. He spent a few days a week helping out at the center, because he wanted to give back because the Center had helped him with his problems with addiction.

"Anyway, Teddy, I need a favor from you", Raul said, remembering and getting back to the purpose of his call.

"Sure Raul, how can I help you?" asked his old friend.

"I will need a ride to Sunday Services at Broken Lives this weekend. Can you or another member of the church help me with that?"

"Sure, I think I can. But if I can't, I will arrange with the guys for one of them to assist you", Teddy promised.

"Alright thanks. If and when you arrange it, call this number and ask for Cheryl. She can give me your reply".

The two friends hung up the phone and Raul waited for Cheryl to return. While waiting he thought about how God works. Was he being shown the many levels of suffering experienced by his clients who have undergone homelessness, by now being homeless himself. Raul was sixty-two and though not young, he was not as old as some people who have undergone homelessness at a very old age. He wondered how many of the homeless have ended up dying on the streets. This thought pricked his senses. The whole concept of the consequences of homelessness benefitted some vile, corrupt individuals. Perhaps greedy doctors who wanted to perform expensive organ transplants for wealthy people desperate to extend their lives at the expense of an innocent person who is homeless. Raul had recently read a braille book about the story of corrupt and illegal organ transplant operations being done on non consenting poor people. Can such wickedness be promoting such wide spread homelessness in this country? And what about other countries? Is this now very prevalent in the world? Greed motivating vast numbers of transplant operations. "No, I can't believe people could be so vile and heartless", Raul tried to reason. At that moment Cheryl came back into the room and asked Raul,

"Were you able to reach the ones that you wanted to connect with?"

"Yes, thank you Cheryl. Everything has been arranged".

"There is some more coffee ready in the kitchen, perhaps you would like a second cup?"

"Yes that sounds fine, again thank you. Could you see me back to the dayroom?"

"Certainly, and then I will bring you that coffee, come let us go".

Together they walked back to the dayroom, where more residents of the Shelter had entered and now there was a game of Spades being played by four young men near the room's window. A group of small children were gathered in front of a large television placed in the center of the room. Raul could hear the sound of a commercial coming from the television and also the noisey chatter of the children in the room. He smiled at the sound of their young voices, excited as they each wanted to make their voices be heard among the voices of a new group that they weren't familiar with. Each trying to get a point across, some not being heard among the large group. Wistfully Raul thought of the quiet he had formerly at 101 Wassail and the now loud cacophony of sound being heard in this present surroundings. Walking over to the sofa with Cheryl guiding him, he sat down and she went for more coffee.

NETTIE AND THE KIDS

Fearful about leaving her kids back at the shelter alone, Nettie took them with her to go to Springfield Memorial Hospital's Morgue. Being directed by a hospital porter, she and the kids went to the lower level of the Hospital, in the East Wing, and were directed by the morgue attendant where they could go to view Louise's body. Reluctantly Nettie asked the attendant if he could watch her little ones while she went to see her mother. She told her kids to stay in the front main room for visitors and to be quiet while she was gone. Led by another attendant, she entered a cold sterile room, in back of the morgue. Approaching a wall of drawers, the attendant pulled out one and there on the drawer slab laid her mother. Nettie's breath stopped momentary and she peered with anguish at her poor mom, resting quietly in momentary sleep. Nettie kept that thought in mind as she remembered her mother teaching from the bible, John Chapter five, verse twenty one (John 5:21)

"for just as the father raises the dead, and gives them life, even so the Son gives life to whom he pleased to give it".

Nettie also remembered her mother quoting Isaiah 25:7,

"On this mountain the Lord Almighty will prepare a feast of

meats and the finest wines. On this mountain he will destroy the shroud that covers all nations; he will swallow up death forever."

With a heavy heart, Nettie broke down and wept. The tears flowing as if they would never stop. On and on, she cried, an endless pouring out of her pain. Then a gentle presence stood by her and she heard her mother's voice,

"I tell you the truth, whoever hears my word and believes him who sent me has eternal life and will not be condemned; he has crossed over from death to life. I tell you the truth, a time is coming and has now come when the dead will hear the voice of the son of God and those who hear will live".

As if strengthened by her mother's voice, Nettie straightened up with courage and determination; she knew she would see her mother again, filled with new life promised by God. Turning she thanked the morgue attendant who had remained and quietly watched her grief.

"I am so sorry for your lost, may God protect you and comfort you", he declared.

"Thank you, yes he has done that already. Bless you for your kindness". Where had the words come from, she wondered. It had been a long time since she had acknowledged God or his presence in her life. Through the years of her marriage she couldn't recall a time that she had taken her concern about the course her marriage was taking to God in prayer or read a bible as she had been so fond of doing as a child. She had learned to read at an early age, enjoying books as much as her older sibling, her brother Bob, who was always an avid reader.

Back in the main front part of the morgue, Nettie walked to her kids and told them,

"I saw Grandma and told her, you all love her. She wants you to know that she loves you too. She said she will watch over you guys from Heaven. That is where she is going". Her children started crying and Nettie hushed them gently.

"No you mustn't cry. Grandma wants you to be brave and not worry. You will see her when God brings you to heaven later", Nettie tried to comfort them.

"Right now, we have to get back to the shelter to get something to eat. On our way I am going to stop and get you guys some candy".

"Can I get some licorice?" Jeremy asked, temporary forgetting his tears for Grandma, now focused on his favorite candy treat; Nettie smiled and assured him that was possible and then she and the kids left the morgue after she thanked the morgue attendant for watching her kids. Together, the kids now a little bit less sad, anticipating the candy promised by their mother, walked beside Nettie, skipping to keep up with her. Outside in the cold, winter air, feeling chilled, Nettie looked worriedly at her kids and wondered if they were feeling the cold as much as she was. Pushing forward, she continued to the end of the block and looked around. She didn't see a store where she could get the candy she had promised the kids. A hospital doctor was walking towards her with rapid steps.

"Excuse me, Sir. Do you know if there is a nearby supermarket?" Nettie stopped him with her question.

Looking at her and then the kids, who were watching him

intensely, as young children often look at adults, the doctor considered her question and then said,

"Well, I believe there is a C-Town Supermarket. But, to think about it, I believe it might be about ten blocks from here, up this same street". He pointed in the direction he was referring to up the street and shifted the textbook he was carrying in his hand. Nettie looked at the book and saw that it was a textbook on Family Medical Practice. Alarmed, at once, she suddenly realized she hadn't called Ken to tell him about Louise's death. He should know that his children's Grandmother had died.

"Oh, my goodness! How could I forget?" She thought and then realized that she hadn't called Glen either. Had she become so used to managing on her own and also in not trusting a man, that she neglected to call her former husband and Glen, to not only inform them but to get help that she so desperately needed now. The thought almost brought tears to her eyes again. Thanking the doctor she pulled out her cell phone from her bag and called Ken. The phone rang and within seconds, Ken answered the phone.

"Good morning, Nettie", Ken's voice immediately made Nettie tense, but with control she forced herself to say, "I have something to tell you".

"Yes, what is it?" Ken said a little bit indifferently.

Nettie, indignant by Ken's coldness, took a deep breath, then went on.

"It's about my mother. There was a fire in our apartment building and...." trying to remain calm, Nettie whispered, "She's dead, Ken. She and Jeremy got trapped in her bedroom during the fire. She managed to throw Jeremy down to the firemen from her bedroom window but lost her footing as she tried to climb out and fell", Nettie managed to tell him.

"Is that Daddy?" Nettie and Ken's oldest child, Marie, asked Nettie.

"SH," Nettie gently told her.

"Oh, my God", Ken blurted out in astonishment at the news.

"The kids are all safe. We are staying at the Blue Cross Homeless Shelter located at 1991 Sullivan Street.

"Nettie, I am so sorry. Your poor mother. Do you need help to arrange her funeral?" Ken asked, sounding genuinely sincere. Nettie felt herself almost break at the sincerity in his voice.

"No, I think I can manage that. I will call you later, after I have made the arrangements. I have to go now", she informed him.

"Ok Nettie, tell the kids, Daddy will be there soon. I......." Ken stammered unsurely. His words resounding in Nettie's ears, as she said "good bye" and ended the call. Marie whined when she realized her mom had ended the call without letting her speak to her daddy. Again Nettie told her to "sh". Now Nettie called Glen to tell him the news. He was also shocked at what she told him.

"Where are you now, honey? I am off from work today. Can I come to be with you and the kids?"

"I am on my way to C-Town Supermarket which is near Springfield Memorial Hospital. Do you think you could meet us there? Do you know where it is?" She asked.

"Don't worry, I'll be there. Traffic is not bad at this time of day, so it shouldn't take me long to get there".

They said their good-byes and Ann told the kids they had to go. They walked up the street towards the C-Town Supermarket, bravely trying to forget the cold, Nettie sung her favorite song, "Born Free" to her children and delighted they joined in singing the words in their little voices with childish energy. Their words, omitting some of the lyrics. But nonetheless, they all were now in a happy mood, not even conscious of the cold, as they sung the song over and over again on their march to the supermarket.

As Nettie and the kids song forcefully with all their energy, Nettie's cell phone rang loudly and the little family stopped singing as Nettie answered the call.

"Yes, who is calling?", Nettie asked hesitantly, wondering if it was Ken calling back.

"Hello, is this Nettie Morgan?", a woman's voice questioned.

"Yes, who is calling?", Nettie responded.

"Ms Morgan, this is Johnson Life Insurance Company, returning your call inquiring about your mother's life insurance policy. Is this a good time to talk to you about your mother's policy?"

"I am not home, but you can tell me what you need to tell me and if I have to write something down, I can call you back when I get home", Nettie explained.

"Great, I would first like to say I am deeply sorry for your loss."

"Thank you for your kind word", Nettie said.

"You are welcome, my dear" the insurance agent said. "Your mother has name you and your children as the beneficiaries of her policy. It is for three million dollars. She also carried a smaller policy for other family members. We can discuss where to locate her other relatives with you later. She wanted her large policy to go to her child, you, and her grandchildren. She has it divided equally among you and the kids."

The woman continued talking but Nettie had stopped listening in a state of astonishment she repeated the number, three million dollars to herself. "Moma, thank you so much, my sweet Moma, I love you. The kids and I are going to be alright. I am going to buy that beautiful house you and I talked about" she whispered. With the special gift her mother had given her and her kids, Nettie envisioned a future of security for them and with new energy she led her children in singing again; this time they sung "Amazing Grace" with harmony.

THE DEMONS AND ARSONISTS

With great anger, Abaddon circling over Nettie and her kids, wanted to charge at them and rip them with his sharp talons.

"Why are they singing?" he screeched in rage. "They are supposed to be devastated. What madness is this?" He thundered, his voice vibrating over the throng of flying demons surrounding him, all of them anxiously waiting for his command, but Abaddon was silent, seething with a powerful urge to inflict deadly harm again. His horde of demons sensing his desire, quivered in excitement, greedy for more action, Expectingly they waited. Would Abaddon give a command to annihilate another life? They all knew Louise's death had not satisfied Abaddon. It had been whispered among them that her soul was now with God "The Almighty and that fact resonated clearly throughout their ranks. Another saint, destined for eternal life. Their enjoyment, the night of the fire at 101 Wassail Avenue, was now dampen. The demonic enthusiasm, now not as fulfilling, as they had hoped, stung their pride; their false belief of a high opinion of themselves. If they and Abaddon had not made wretched this little family, lead by Nettie, how could they hope to win the final battle against the Almighty, especially since they did not know when that battle would take place. Like the Almighty, they had prophets too, but of cause as stated in the Almighty's Holy word, their prophets were false prophets so how could they reliably count on them with their planning for that future day; the final day of the apocalypse. The final revelation given of God destroying Evil. If at this stage (and who knows, the present day could well be ions before the final battle), if they couldn't win in a small scrimmage, what was the likelihood that they would ultimately defeat the "I Am". Abaddon also felt this chill of his and all demons eventful defeat and tried to ignore it; but the chill was always present. It's shivers, a bone deep constant reminder.

"Let us head elsewhere. We have more work to do with the arsonists". The command, a high pitched cry, given by Abaddon, pierced the ears of the other demons and not following too closely to Abaddon, they all, rose in strict formation and left the area, no longer concerned with Nettie and her children.

Back at the meeting hall, the arsonists were still surrounded and influenced by demons who were told to linger back and make sure the arsonists would continue their exploits (secretly given to them under the directions of Abaddon's demonic whisperings and the whisperings of his auxilliary army of subverter demons he had left in place at the hall). Leon "the Lion" convinced he was the only force in control, had no knowledge of Abaddon's interference. Today he was excited about the lack of any real preparation or hindrance against his plans, as demonstrated by all the success of his arsonists. But he now wanted another strategy to be implemented. He implored all his brightest recruits in the ranks to brainstorm with a mighty endeavor, aiming for brilliance, with all the talent that their intellect was capable of, the goal; their annihilation immediately of this pesky thing called American Capitalism. In the Lion's mind it represented society's ultimate ruin. With all the filth it produced. Under it, any man was able to produce and distribute whatever product to the masses. Examples of the immorality it produced was evident everywhere.

The other night Leon had witness, anew it's deep depth of depravity. He had come home after spending hours mustering the members of the "Brotherhood" to give out new orders. After heating a pot of Chilli taken from his refrigerator, he spooned out a bowlful and sat down on his comfortable blue recliner that was positioned directly in front of his fifty-five inch television. Taking his remote, he surfed the channels, looking for something to watch. Abruptly, his finger stopped clicking the remote control. He felt an intense surge of blood to the sphincter muscle of his bladder. He inhaled sharply. On the television screen was a darken room of immense size and in spite of the dimness of the light in the room, the naked bodies of men and women could be seen and were embraced in various positions, engaged in feverish sex with each other. Outraged, beyond his mind's ability to comprehend, this present affront to morality quickened his blood and he felt a vein pulse on his forehead. He breathed deeply and incredulous at America's wickedness, he watched the orgy as it progressed, with unrestrained twisting and explosive orgasms after orgasms in the writhing bodies of the participants within this room of sin. They all had ecstatic contentment visible on their faces. Some relaxed after their climaxes only to stiffen as wave after wave of another climax vibrated in their lower bodies.

Leon's breathe quicken and trying to fight the start of his own experiencing of a slow orgasm, he jumped up and rushed to the television and turned it off. Fighting his physical response of intense sexual arousal, he cursed America and its avaricious tendencies of allowing anything on T.V. or other media devices; all in the name of making a buck. What about the children? It was only nine o'clock on a week night. Any child could have turned on the T.V. and saw what little eyes shouldn't see. He thought of his Christian grandmother who warning his mother to be careful of sin's enticement, often quoted from Ecclesiastes Chapter three verse seventeen, of the Bible,

"God will bring to judgement both the righteous and the wicked, for there will be a time for every activity, a time for every deed"

KWUAME AND JOSHUA

It was 7:00 pm and once again Kwuame had returned to visit Joshua at the hospital. He hoped that he could this time, be able to express to Mr. Rosenshein, the gratitude he felt. Arriving on the I.C.U. unit he quickly walked towards Joshua's room; entering he was surprised to see that Shannah was once again there. But he reflected, of course she would be here. She was totally devoted to her husband.

"Why Kwuame, how good of you to return so soon. Thank you" she said effectionally, then turned abruptly as she heard,

"Wait, wait....please".

It was Joshua's voice, choking and straining as he made his plea. She and Kwuame turned and watched in amazement as Joshua lifted his head in their direction. Kwuame walked quickly to the bed and sat down. He reached for Joshua's hand and grasping it tightly said.

"Thank you so much Mr. Rosenshein. Thank you for saving my life. Why did you risk your life for me?" Kwuame again voiced his utter bewilderment at Joshua's sacrifice.

"Pekuach nefesh, it is the highest Mitzvah in Judaism" Joshua weakly mumbled. Then breathed deeply. "It means the highest good deed done, the saving and preservation of life. During the Korean War, a Black Soldier came back for me during a foot patrol. I had fallen into a pit. He rescused me". Joshua took a few more deep breathes.

"I feel all creation has a purpose. I think about God's creation" Ants. Exactly why did God create them? You observe them and I reflect that what is apparent is that they are hard working, industrious, with a single mindness, strictly devoted and obedient in working for their Queen Ant. I say "wow", has God created them to show by their very existence and habits, how God demands that we follow him, with strict obedience to his directive and with oneness of purpose; to love him and love others". Joshua's words seem to even flabbergast himself.

Shannah and Kwuame looked as Joshua collapsed back down onto his bed and drifted off into sleep. His extraordinary effort to say these words were incredible to them. Walking over to his side, Shannah leaned over and kissed Joshua's forehead.

KWUAME AND NAT

The next day after visiting Mr Rosenhein at the Hospital, Kwuame was even more troubled about the pressing thoughts swirling through his brain. In a few minutes his uncle Khaalig and Nat were going to meet with a friend of Khaalig to discuss the organization Khaalig had told him about, "Brother's United". But at this moment, Kwuame could only think about Joshua. He had looked as if he might die at any moment, as he had finished his unexpected surreal remarks to Kwuame. Said as from some hypnotic trance; the words flowing rapidly as if guided by God. It had scared Kwuame at first, until he considered the message in the words. The simplicity of the message, similar to how Jesus had taught his disciples and the crowds who had come to hear him. Kwuame had been told this by his mother. She said Jesus's ministry was primarily taught through reciting parables. These are short stories demonstrating moral lessons or codes.

What was Joshua's remarks? Kwuame pondered. He had said that God demands that we follow him with obedience and "oneness of purpose, to love him and others".

Suddenly, Kwuame jumped up and made a mad dash to the bathroom, showered and brushed his teeth, anxiously aware of the time, quickly approaching the time of Khaalig's meeting. Quickly dressing and putting his wallet in his pants pocket and picking up his keys, he rushed out of his aunt's apartment. He and his parents were now living with his aunt and uncle in a close proximity to their old apartment at 101 Wassail Avenue. The family group were relieved to have this option available to them at their sudden condition of homelessness. It was an unbelievable blessing not available to the masses of other homeless communities across the world; the help and availability of another home with relatives after losing one's home. The tragedy of homelessness; the lack of a needed shelter to protect oneself from harm; harm caused by any situation; extreem weather conditions and possible assault that could be caused by lack of needed physical shelter, and then to not be able to turn to anyone to help you in your helpless, vulnerable condition. As Kwuame tried to reach the coffee shop at 1901 Sullivan Street in time for the meeting, he thought about how so many of his former neighbors were at the Blue Cross Shelter. He wondered how long they would be able to stay there. Khaalig had said that would be one of the things they would discuss today.

Within a very short time Kwuame arrived at "Coffee and Sweets", the coffee shop where Khaalig was having his meeting. Walking through the entrance door, Kwuame was able to immediately locate Khaalig sitting at a back table talking with Nat plus two other guys. He walked swiftly over to them and sat down.

"Hey guys, I hope you don't mind me sitting in on this session?", he asked and greeted everyone.

"Kwuame, this is Tony Dawson and Filippe Ortez, guys meet

my nephew, Kwuame". Everyone smiled and acknowledged each other and shook hands.

"Okay, here's what you missed, Kwuame. We were discussing the severity of the homeless situation in this country. Other guys from our group are working on getting numbers and data about this troubling pattern elsewhere in the world" Khaalig explained and said, "according to information I've obtained, two hundred twenty-five people lost their lives from sleeping and living out on the streets last year in the winter. I'm sure the numbers are high at other times during the year too".

"I definitely would suppose so. I mean, hot weather can be deadly too, especially if you have to live out doors", Kwuame added.

"I can't stand when the air conditioner turns off during summer. It's a mother..." Khaalig stopped with a remark.

"Image your grandparents in such a situation or little kids who don't understand why you won't take them from out of the cold or heat".

Nat had been quiet and so had Tony Dawson up to this point. Now Tony Dawson spoke.

"called a Christian Hot Line about the availability of a room at a Christian affiliated homeless shelter. She said that there was but a person could only stay there for thirty days. She also said that the Salvation Army offers beds for seven nights and then you would have to pay five dollars a night to stay there after that period".

"Man, you must be kidding", Nat exclaimed.

"No, I kid you not. Then she had the nerve to ask me for a donation. I kindly told her that she might want to ask some of our billionaires or millionaires in this country for some money. I told her she could also check the government's spending, that maybe they have some extra money floating around", Tony said, obviously fed up with the whole situation.

"By the way, that is one of the areas I was going to check into. Exactly where has the money from last year's budget for the government gone towards?" Khaalig asked.

"There is such a thing mentioned in the budget concerning "Effective Stewardship".

"What is that?" Nat inquired.

"Well, basically, wait...let me read from the government's statement, what it says about it. I wrote it down yesterday, it states 'effective stewardship of taxpayer funds is a crucial responsibility, from preventing fraud to maximizing impact', it says further, that, 'taxpayer's dollars must go to effective programs that efficiently produce results...and also that savings could be achieved through the prevention of improper payments alone'.". Khaalig smiled then lean forward. "Now get this. How much do you think we could save over a decade by eliminating and preventing improper payments to the C.I.A. and FBI ALONE?"

Nat shook his head, failing to imagine how much. Tony and Kwuame looked baffled and shook their heads also.

"Well, get this. The government could save $139 Billion. Can you imagine!!"

"Holy shit", you realize how that money could be put to good use?" Kwuame said,

"Man I am glad I came today. Guys we have to definitely check further and see how we can turn things around. Make a complete rotation of a cycle of events, bring about a complete change in conditions here in this country". He said with excitement.

"Slow down, warrior." Khaalig laughed. "We need to mobilize people. Wake them up from their hypnotic slumber. That means drawing other men into our circle and reaching across our sex to get the aid of some females too. So I suggest we think of renaming our organization to "Brothers and Sisters United". Have a membership drive to help not only get new members but also the financial help we will need. I want it to be a Christian Fellowship. Are you guys okay with that?"

Kwuame looked uncertain about the wisdom of that. Maybe a lot of guys are not going to want to be a part of that. A large number of brothers of his race thought Christianity was a White Man's religion, he thought. Other points were swirling in his head. But thinking of his parents beliefs and what had just happened to him; his rescue from possibily dying, being implemented by the kindness of a Jewish man, caused him to consider that maybe the new organization did need to be conceived by the help of God.

He nodded his head in agreement to Khaalig's request and the other two guys also agreed on the matter. With input from everyone they eventually roughed out a plan of action and a date to get others to come and participate in this new endeavor. Phone calls were made and plans further discussed. After about two hours the group decided to end this meeting and encouraged by the excitement they all felt, they shook hands again and vowed to immediately get to work on their plans. As a group, they exited the coffee shop with determination and a commitment for change.

THE LION

At the same time Khaalig and Kwuame along with Nat and Tony, were discussing and trying to formulate their plans for change, a radical change in society, The "Lion" Leon was across town in the same meeting hall of the arsonists, addressing the members of his group. His words thundering and heavy with contempt once again. As always the room was hushed and listening attentively to his words.

"I believe perhaps this whole country needs to become homeless. Starting with all worthless politicians; our so called political leaders and all our governing agencies. Perhaps the indignity of not having an adequate paying job for providing money to pay for rent and to feed your family, should be allowed to be inflicted on them." the crowd roared in agreement. Many in the audience had experienced being homeless at one time.

"The pain of homelessness should be inflicted on smug people who have the benefit of a good paying job and help when they need it; maybe they should experience homelessness because of suddenly becoming jobless because of losing their car or it getting burned, and now they don't have a way to get to that high paying job." He stopped and waited a full minute for that fact to stir his audience. "Would this awaken the masses? Would this awaken people to the injustice impinged on honest hardworking people who are not getting paid fairly by this corrupt system in America, that allows for greedy people like big Pharmaceutical Companies and Music Producers to take advantage of people". He sneered in contempt. His face hardened with seething anger.

"To have so much corruption that is brought on by white superiority and racism or by greedy businessmen who don't pay decent wages to their workers". These words vibrated throughout the hall and heads nodded in agreement.

"Should their comfort be allowed to exist and flourish with no concern by our politicians who apparently haven't done a dame thing to reverse this?"

"Here's a thought, that might awaken the person of the mindset of the belief that you have to either have a disability or a mental illness to become homeless. Homelessness can affect all of us in this present country. And the outrage and despair of a homeless person in a shelter that can lead them to be violent or seek drug addiction to blunt their miserable existence in filthy shelters and the outrage about the shelter's workers not giving a damn about their condition; is indeed enough to invoke violence".

His delivery hit home and many realized that their passion was renewed. His description of what they have felt towards their oppressors were validated by Leon. "The Lion", was echoed throughout the hall and clapping of hands accentuated his message.

"So, let us not be so arrogant and go home to our comfortable beds and drink water freely and eat a cooked meal and forget that the homeless do not have this privilege". Again there was more clapping.

"Let us not stop until the right to have sufficient housing and a job, is every man's right. Not to be discussed indefinitely for years. No, I say. EMPHATICALLY NO!!!," again there was more thunderous applause.

"No it has to be immediate. No more allowing these victims to suffer. To be organ donors for the rich and powerful" There was a hush at this stated atrocity.

"No, their lives matter. We must not wait for change. But we must demand it at once." This was meet with silence by everyone in the room.

"Demand that we will not wait. No more lives lost in the cold of winter or the heat of summer. Our lives matter. Change now or never. Everyone dies." He roared like the jungle animal he was nick-named for "The Lion"

"We will all have homes or none of us will have homes or cars to go to fancy jobs that will no longer be there." Again there was an eruption of fierce clapping and cheering.

"No longer will we be money for wealthy doctors. One rich man must lose almost all his material wealth (but not family or pets, but his material wealth, his money). He must be left with just enough to make immediate arrangement to shelter millions with what he has left. And if by his example, other people of wealth who do not pitch in and help provide immediately, homes for the homeless (not years from now, not months from now, but immediately), they too should be left poor." Everyone applauded again loudly and endlessly.

"If these empty homes that real estate agents greedily hold onto in expectation of a fat paycheck, don't become immediately offered to the homeless until permanent homes, that they can afford, becomes available; then all in this country must become homeless. There are empty apartments across this country; empty hotels across this country; everyone must be filled with the homeless. Their families notified of where they are and help of some substance given to them". Once again this message was thundered by Leon.

"No one will have a place to live if this is not done. No politician will have a home or job if they don't start (after the example of that first rich man) to enact legislations that are funded immediately and funds distributed to the homeless; if not done then all guns shops must be burned. All leaders, all people must lose their homes (but protect the innocent and the pets, none are to be harmed). Let everyone finally understand homelessness. Let every rich man's bank account show insufficient funds. Let this be documented that this actually happens. We know where they live, where they eat. Where they get their food. All will be burned down and that will be immediately. No one spared". Some people in the crowded room looked at each other and showed concern on their faces.

Soon after his speech all the different divisions of his group met in their individual groups and went over the demanded directions given by "the Lion". Who would the first rich man be? Who would serve as an example to the world of the Brotherhood serious requirement of decency that must be shown towards the homeless. The man of wealth, not to be allowed to own multiple cars and homes, while the poor suffered. This man's money must be taken; stocks taken; homes taken; cars taken; jewels taken; gold taken; nothing left to him but enough to help the homeless.

With an urgent plan formalized, they set out to implement it. The wealthy man was selected, calls were made to other countries, bank accounts were hacked into. Workers were placed at the man's various residences and the okay was given to search for the innocent and all pets. All were taken off the properties and then the places were quickly burnt. The many cars burnt. The night was filled with burning.

JOHN AND MANNY

Manny tried calling Tamara's number again and got no answer. Frustrated, he put his phone in his pant's pocket and entered the Genesis Awakement Center. He went down the hall towards the room where his group therapy session was held. Coming out of the room was Mr. Solomon.

"Hello, Mr Solomon, how are you?"

"Fine Manny, I'm glad I ran into you. I just placed a note on the door to let everyone know that the group session will have to be rescheduled".

"What! Why is it being rescheduled?"

"Well, unfortunately your counselor Raul will not be here today, there was a fire in his apartment building and it burned completely. He is now in a homeless shelter, the Blue Cross Shelter" Mr. Solomon informed Manny.

"Gee, that's terrible. I hadn't heard about it. I think I will go visit him. Maybe my friend Tamara, who lives in his building is there too. I haven't been able to reach her. Thanks Mr Solomon".

Manny hurried back through the Center long hallway and exited the building. Outside he tried to remember where the Blue Cross Shelter was located. Reaching into his backpack he pulled out his map of Brooklyn and carefully searching it he found the street he believed the center was located on. Looking closely at the map he determined that he could take a bus to the destination. Once again he pulled out his phone and dialed information. Giving the operator the name of the shelter, she then confirmed it's location. Thanking her, he hung up and strolled to the bus stop.

The bus ride was not a long one and he soon arrived at Sullivan Street where he departed from the bus. Quickly he entered 1991 Sullivan and going to the front desk asked if a Mr. Raul and Tamara Ramsey were staying at the shelter.

"Well, let me see. There is a Tamara Ramsey and Ann Ramsey who have recently been registered here. If this is who you are looking for I will have to have you wait here while I let the workers inside know you are asking to see her. Also there is a Raul Vasquez in our books. Do you want me to notify him too?"

"yes, thank you, I would appreciate that".

The receptionist then dialed a number and waited to be connected.

"There is a .....I'm sorry, I didn't get your name".

"My name is Manny".

"All right. UMM, the person name is Manny. He wishes to see a Tamara Ramsey and a Mr Raul Vasquez", the receptionist informed the other person at the end of the line.

"Yes, okay I will tell him that". She turned back to Manny.

"Ms Tamara and her mother are not here now. But Raul will be out presently to speak with you. There are seats and tables in the room to the right of you. You can wait in there if you wish".

"Thank you, I will do that". He went into the room and sat

down. Looking around he wasn't impressed with what he saw. Torn wallpaper was on the walls (he hated wallpaper so he immediately frowned) and the curtains at the window did not even match the wall paper. "Some one has bad taste or maybe they are blind like Raul", he thought, still sizing the room up and finding it lacking in any warmth or apparent hospitality. "What a dismal place" he thought. It was enough to make you want to drink" He noticed a sign on the wall advertising a blood donation drive which was suppose to be given at the center tomorrow.

"Wow, you lose your home and then someone has the nerve to want to get your blood too", Manny whistled loudly to accent his remark, then shook his head in amazement at the vulture mentality of the world. Then he saw his old friend Raul being led into the room with the help of a shelter worker.

"Hey Raul, how are you? Gee I'm sorry about the fire", he expressed softly.

"Thank you for saying that Manny. I am as well as can be expected, under the circumstance. Didn't see this coming" Raul chuckled.

"Do you know what has happened to Tamara and her mother?"

"They are fine son, they are here at the shelter too. I know they went out earlier but I don't think they are back yet".

"Wow, Thank God. I was worried about all of you. By the way what happened to your neighbor John, the paraplegic? Did he get out too?"

"You know son, I don't know. He is not here. They probably have him at Springfield Memorial because of his condition. I completely forgot about him. My goodness!!!"

Manny and Raul spent about an hour talking then Manny felt an urgency to go to the hospital to check and see if John was there.

"Raul, I feel inclined to investigate and find out what has happened to John. If you don't mind, I'm going to leave now and do that".

"That's great, go ahead and thanks for checking on me. Tell the guys at Rap I hope to see them soon".

Both men hugged each other then Manny departed. Back on the bus he headed to Spring Field Memorial. Thirty minutes later he was at the hospital information desk for visitors. Standing before the desk he asked about a patient named John Peterson and waited while the receptionist checked on a screen placed in front of him.

"Mr Peterson is in Room 304 on the third floor. Here is a visitor's pass". She handed Manny the cardboard pass and he thanked her. Reaching John's hospital door he gently knocked on it.

"Who is there?" John said. Opening the door Manny walked in. John was lying in a hospital bed that had been raised for him.

"Hi, I don't know if you remember me, but Raul, your old neighbor introduced me to you some time ago. Do you remember?"

John looked closely at Manny and recognition appeared in his eyes.

"Yes, I remember you. What brings you Here?"

Slowly Manny walked over to a chair and sat down. "I don't know myself really", Manny smiled, unsure how to proceed.

"I guess I wanted to see if you needed anything? If someone has been to see you, a family member or friend?". John stared as if he had been asked the stupidest question in the world. He said nothing, just continued to look at Manny.

"Well, I guess my answer would be no judging by your look. Look man, I don't want to intrude on your solitude but you know, sometimes it helps to just have another person around". He stopped and looked around the room. It was small like most hospital rooms and noticeably cold as well.

"So do you have relatives living in New York?", he asked John.

"No", John said automatically, then looking embarrassed said, "I come from Tennessee. My parents are dead and I haven't heard from my sister in years. She doesn't even know I have been wounded in the Army", he said as if the words were waiting for someone to bring them out.

"Man, I'm sorry. We all need family. Even if they aren't the best relationship, I guess", he said thinking of his mom. Then shook that thought away, remembering the advice given to him by Raul. Anyway, it all was just a matter of perception. How one allowed himself to view the world. He now wanted a positive outlook, with no foolish grudges linkering in his soul. Smiling, he grabbed John hands and squeezed them tightly. John found himself squeezing Manny's hands in return. Slowly the guys started talking.

"You know, I had been isolated myself. Even though I have a family I am a recovering addict", Manny told John.

"For some time I have been angry and allowed that anger to grow and eventually consume me. I started drinking, using drugs occasionally. I felt unable to stop. Ran with the wrong crowd. Isolated myself at home from my family. Keep my bedroom door closed and played my music loudly, trying to drown out the world. Only wanted to be left alone. Yes I know loneliness and I recognized it in you", Manny smiled gently and again squeezed John's hand.

John closed his eyes and breathed heavily. Manny went on,

"It took some time but I eventually sorted help after an old lady in my apartment house where I used to live, before my brother brought the house my mom, sisters and I live in now, prayed for me". John calmly listened to this new friend of his. He realized he wanted him as a friend.

"This old lady knew I was lying to her about needing her to give me money for food and she asked if she could pray for me. I let her and have not regretted it since. I stopped taking and indulging in drugs and alcohol. Got myself a job and into treatment at the Genesis Awakement Center", he continued to smile encouragely at John.

"The whole program is excellent. You know you might be able to attend if you want. They work with all type of individuals and have a wide range of classes, offering many subjects. Besides counseling, they offer writing, painting, photography. Gee as I've said, a wide range of classes to not only help the mind but to also help the creativity of their clients. So much is offered", Manny informed John.

John's eyes lit up for the first time in a long time.

"You said they offer painting?"

"Yes, all types. Oil painting, watercolor, arcylic and pastels. Did you paint before your accident?"

"Not for a long time. I used to love doing it before I started playing football, then I kinda thought it was sissy I guess", he smiled sheepishly.

"Man, are you crazy? There are some quite wealthy male painters And some or maybe the majority of the famous painters were male, I believe", Manny told John, looking incredulous at his new friend. They both started laughing.

"I'm going to see if the staff can reach out to you. By the way, all you guys are going to need a new home. I've heard talk of a new group of Christians working at finding homes for the homeless and people with mental problems too. I am going to talk to my friend Tamara about a former ballerina who is homeless and mentally ill. My friend Tamara, who was one of your neighbors, talks about this homeless former dancer constantly. I want to help her get housing and treatment".

John seem very interested, in fact quite interested and realized he wanted to be part of this group.

"What is this group's name?", he asked.

"It is called "Brothers and Sisters United". We want to reach out to the group of arsonists that have been burning buildings here and elsewhere we have found out. Their leader wants immediate homes for the homeless and is dangerously intent on making everyone homeless if homelessness is not addressed. The Christain organization I was told, found this out because one of them attended the arsonist meeting where they discussed it".

John was captivated by everything he heard. No longer willing to sit alone by himself, he felt a surge of hope for his life for the first time since his accident. He now thought of homelessness, he realized for the first time. The thought of not being indoors, protected from rain, especially those torrential downpours that occur occasionally, or the swift gale of a severe snow storm, or the scorching rays of a blistering hot summer day, had never actually crossed his mind. He felt a deep shame at his lack of empathy for these people everyone seemed to have ignored for so long, for so many years. Other awakings to the realities of his so vastly inaccurate perceptions he previously had before leaving Tennessee and going into the Army; about the true nature of the various racial groups that make of mankind, stun him. He had seen through looking, out his apartment's windows, how alike his own race, his neighbors were at Wassail Street.

The afternoon slowly went on and the guys became permanent friends, and Manny left after visiting hours were ended. Early the next day, Manny took the day off from work and was one of first customers at Michael's Arts and Crafts; he had decided last night that he had to buy some art supplies for his new friend John. He felt an urgency to get the supplies to John today. He had to ask the advice of one of the store's employees to help him decide what to get for John. He left with two large canvas broads, a box of ten acrylic paint colors, a value pack of assorted paint brushes and a pack of number two pencils, and an eraser. Satisfied with his purchases, he rushed to the hospital to see John and spend the day with him. He had heard from Tamara and had told her of his visit with John yesterday and about his plans to visit John today. She said it was great that he wanted to help John.

Arriving at John's hospital room within a short time, he found John staring off at the room's close window.

"Glad to see that you are awake. I got a surprise for you. I hope you like it. I kind of believe you will", Manny smiled his usual dazzling grin, and placed his bag of purchases from Michael's Arts and Crafts on John's bedside table. John's eyes lit up when he saw what Manny had brought. His grin at that moment equaled Manny's.

"Man, you did,'t have to do this, but thank you". He eagerly set to work on painting a portrait of two lions, male and female, with their foreheads touching in an obvious display of their affection for each other.

"Wow, that's a masterpiece. I had no idea you could paint that well, but I did feel an urgency to get you these supplies today", Manny said, in complete awe of John's artistic ability.

"I definitely am going to hook you up at the Genesis Awakement Center's art class. And I expect a commission on all you produce and sell there", Manny laughed. Again the two new friends talked and shared their enjoyment of fellowship's goodness.

ANN

It was near midnight and Ann was still awake laying in her cot at the Blue Cross Shelter. Tamara was softly snoring, in the cot next to her, reminding Ann of how as a baby she had snored peacefully when Ann and Jack first brought her home from the hospital after her birth. They had watched her sleeping, amazed at this new being that they had created. Ann now thought, "no, the little girl that God had created and lent to us". She smiled and then the whole remembrance of that day rushed back to her. Her solemn vow to God to tell of his goodness, his majesty and wonderful blessings. To write about his love for his children and all of his creation. She now almost sobbed when she realized this is what she was supposed to do in honor of God. She remembered her first attempts to write her novel. The severe headaches she would get and then feeling defeated she gave up trying to write. The years went by and she forgot that vow made that day. Her fear of dying from the pain of those headaches had stopped her. Looking around the Blue Cross Shelter she saw an old desk in a far corner of the room. Getting up, she crossed the floor and sat down at the desk.

As if waiting for her, there was a stack of notebooks and pens on the desk top. Without any fear of the headache that now appeared as before, those many years ago, she picked up a pen and with a steady hand, with the pain now increasing in her head, she swiftly wrote the words, "Somewhere in the mist of time, an old prophet dreamt his dreams. World events, some past, some present, and others yet to come, paraded through the recesses of his mind in vast spectrum of colors. Brilliant, vibrant colors intermingled with soft, fleeting whispers of hue to almost stark black and white images, depicting stories some have known, know and will know. Across millenniums these stories traveled to reach the sleeping prophet.

Letters spread out in front of the prophet's tunnel vision, in black and white, forming patterns of ancient tongues. His eye eyes zoomed closer, trying to decipher the images but the patterns shifted to rise in spirals, moving outwards before compressing together. Inhaling and exhaling the letters into his being, the prophet mumbled the words "in the beginning was the word and the word was with God and the word was God",.....

THE ALPHA AND THE OMEGA

The words flowed from Ann's pen as if already conceived in the universe at God's command. With increasing speed she wrote. The story supported by all that she had either witnessed or learnt over the years. She remembered her drive to help the neighborhood teens when she first started teaching and was assigned to P.S. 67 in the Fort Green Projects. There was a plot of land that was gated attached to the school and one day she got permission from the school's janitor to use the little area to start a garden. She went to the Housing Project's Maintenance Office and borrowed needed tools; hoes and shovels, rakes and the help of the staff to get a wheelbarrow also. She called the Bronx Botanical Gardens and a young White man came to help her and some parents and children plant the garden. Her mentor and friend Ben arrived and planted cabbage along with watermelon seeds in the garden.. Later at the end of the summer the garden had produced a wonderful harvest but someone stole the watermelons.

Ann added this to her outline for her story. Then she thought of the night when she left work late one evening and saw a young man and woman dragging a garbage bag to the large public trash dumpster at the entrance to the Project's Playground Park. Ann had to go through this entrance to get to the Bus Stop she needed at the other end of the Park. This evening the young couple she saw were troubling to her. The woman was sobbing hysterically and the young man looked fierce and threatening. He kept trying to get the woman to shut up. As Ann watched the bag the man carried broke, what emerged looked like human skin. Ann had gasped and then saw the man hurriedly dump the bag and it's contents into the dumpster. Ann hurried out of the park and luckily her bus was waiting at the bus stop. Getting on she sat down and retrieved her cell phone from her bag and called 911. She told the dispatcher what she had seen and where. The bus had a few minutes wait normally before it would pull out. Ann waited during that time to see if she could hear a police siren arriving to check what she had reported. No siren sounded and after awhile the Bus pulled out. Ann reflected on the face of the young woman in the park and on the face of the young addicted mother she had seen a few days ago and the faces of the woman's children. The pain of all these memories raced to her and she put her thoughts of the Crack Cocaine world that most likely was part of the pain on all of those faces she remembered, into her story.

Ann shivered with dismay and like the prophet in her story, silent tears spilled from her eyes.

Printed in the United States
by Baker & Taylor Publisher Services